THE WHISPERING TONGUES

A sumptuous and unputdownable Regency murder mystery

BETH ANDREWS

Sussex Regency Romance Book 3

Joffe Books, London
www.joffebooks.com

First published in Great Britain in 2022

Cover art by Jarmila Takač

ISBN: 978-1-80405-580-9

'Alas, they had been friends in youth;
But whispering tongues can poison truth.'

Christabel, by Samuel Taylor Coleridge

CHAPTER ONE: AN IMPROPER PROPOSAL

'God bless my soul!' Mr Bigg-Wither exclaimed. His wife, who had been half-dozing on the sofa, raised her head in mild concern. He seemed quite agitated.

'What is the matter?' she asked.

His face was pressed so resolutely against the window — which looked out on New King Street below — that he seemed to be attached to it, and his look was one of utter astonishment.

'I do believe,' he flung over his shoulder, 'that Anthea Halliwell has just passed by on the opposite side of the street.'

'Impossible!' His wife sat up abruptly and scurried to join him at the window. She discerned a trim figure retreating at some distance. It was definitely female and quite shapely, even in a woefully antiquated gown. But surely it could not be Miss Halliwell herself. That was unlikely in the extreme. Aside from which, what possible reason could Bath's most infamous recluse have for escaping from her self-imposed incarceration? No. It must be someone else.

'I tell you I am right.'

'Nonsense.' Mrs Bigg-Wither gave a dismissive shrug and returned to her sofa. 'You have had a little too much wine, my dear.'

While they dithered, Anthea was moving with purposeful tread, not insensible of the interest she was exciting from her neighbours, but perfectly indifferent. She acknowledged no one as she passed by, nor was she acknowledged in passing — but still the residents continued to stare and speculate.

It was neither her beauty nor her figure which garnered such avid attention. Spiteful persons might claim that her beauty was sadly faded since the days when she was considered a reigning Toast. In this, however, they were mistaken. It was not her looks which had faded, but her hopes. The blue eyes were as lovely as ever, but the glow was gone from them. The thoughtless optimism of youth had vanished, replaced by a calm resignation. The girlish laughter had retreated, and even smiles were emigres so few and so infrequent that they were scarce remembered by her anymore.

As she approached her destination in nearby Charles Street, just below the southern edge of Bath, her thoughts were going round and round in her head like a whirligig. A revolution was occurring in the lodgings which she shared with her father, Sir Harry Halliwell. What the ultimate effects might be, she could not yet tell. She had always been a dutiful daughter, and circumstances had dictated a more than common dependence upon Sir Harry which she had accepted with good grace rather than unalloyed pleasure. But today a line had been crossed which necessitated a radical break with the past.

The buildings of Charles Street stretched before her on either side like a genteel Palladian canyon, at once comforting and confining, as she rushed headlong toward her fate. Pausing only to avoid a sedan chair supported by two panting chairmen, she crossed the street and stepped boldly up to a dark front door which gave no indication of what sort of person dwelt within.

'Courage,' she whispered to herself before raising her hand to knock.

It was several heartbeats later that the door swung inward. A stout, middle-aged woman stood there, frowning at her in some consternation. Before she could speak, however, a figure appeared just behind her, pushing forward and speaking at the same time.

'Who is it, Mrs Norton?'

The second lady was much younger — barely out of the schoolroom, Anthea would say. She had sparkling dark eyes, much like her father's, was somewhat short but slim enough. Not a beauty, but she had a gamin charm which would only increase with age. She eyed the strange visitor with undisguised curiosity and without a tinge of embarrassment.

'I do not know as yet, Miss,' the housekeeper replied.

'Would you be so good as to tell Mr Rodrigo that Miss Halliwell would like a word with him?'

'Anthea Halliwell!' the girl cried, now frankly staring. 'The hermit of Bath?'

'The very same.' For the first time today, Anthea felt the smallest bubble of amusement welling up within her at this disingenuous remark.

'You cannot be serious,' the young lady objected.

'I assure you that I am she.'

'But you are far too beautiful to be a recluse!' she objected, clearly not intending to flatter but simply stating the obvious.

'Thank you.' Anthea smiled slightly. 'And may I be allowed to enter?'

Belatedly realizing that her unexpected guest was still standing on the outside of the door, the young lady stepped back and motioned her to enter.

'I beg your pardon,' she replied as Anthea entered.

'I shall inform Mr Rodrigo that you are here,' Mrs Norton said, but before she could move in that direction her companion forestalled her.

'No, no!' she insisted. 'Let me tell Papa. This is a most auspicious occasion, after all.'

Anthea did not know quite how to take this remark but shrugged and waited in the hall while the housekeeper took herself off, eager to escape an awkward situation. Left alone,

Anthea glanced at her reflection in an oval mirror placed conveniently near the entrance. It was not a comforting sight. The face which looked back bore the clear signs of the apprehension — not to say desperation — which she felt. Her cheeks were rosy after a brisk walk and her eyes bright, but with anxiety rather than excitement. Her hat, like her gown, was faded and out of fashion. It was no wonder, seeing that it had been some years since she had bought a new outfit, and those she possessed had already been re-fashioned well beyond their intended use.

While she waited, she could plainly hear the voice of the strange young woman as she opened a door at the end of the hallway and sang out: 'Papa, the most beautiful lady in the most hideous gown is here to see you!'

'Miss Halliwell is here?' came the somewhat more muffled response. 'Great God!'

A moment later and the gentleman himself appeared in the hall, advancing rapidly toward her.

'My dear Miss Halliwell,' he said, stopping to execute a brief bow, 'this is an unexpected pleasure indeed.'

'Thank you, sir.' She inclined her head, feeling more than ordinary constraint with the young lady behind him regarding them both with unabashed curiosity. 'I—I hope that you will forgive me for coming unannounced in this way.'

'There is nothing to forgive, ma'am. But please be good enough to accompany me to my study. This young lady,' he added, indicating their interested audience, 'is my daughter, Rachel, who is about to take herself off, if I am not mistaken.'

Rachel executed a neat curtsey to Anthea, poked her tongue out at her papa, and promptly proceeded to do as he had said.

At this point, Mrs Norton reappeared, and Anthea's host requested that she bring some tea for himself and his guest. The older woman did not look as though she approved of her master entertaining strange women in his study, but naturally could not say so. She merely turned on her heel and retired with great dignity.

* * *

Anthea presently found herself seated in a commodious apartment with furnishings more lavish than the simple hall, but not overly ornate. A large mahogany desk dominated the room, flanked by two walls filled with shelves containing hundreds of expensively bound books. Were they merely ornamental, she wondered, or was he indeed a great reader?

She balanced on the edge of a chair which should have been moderately comfortable. Nothing, however, could compensate for the extreme discomfort of her situation. Now that the moment she had been nerving herself for had arrived, she was lost for words to express her ideas. Instead, she gazed silently at the man before her, now sitting quietly behind the desk, darkly silhouetted against a large window.

He looked so foreign suddenly. The onyx-black eyes and hair and the faintly tanned complexion bore what many would call a distinctly Israelite cast, although she was sensible enough to realize that the look — like his exotic-sounding name — was more Spanish than Jewish. He was, she considered, one of the most handsome men of her acquaintance. Even the touch of silver at his temples was oddly attractive. He might be approaching his fortieth year, but he certainly had not assumed the mantle of middle age. His height was not much above average, but his shoulders were broad and his figure exceptionally good.

For several moments he returned her look without comment, until at last he gave a slight cough.

'There is something, perhaps, which you wish to ask me?'

Anthea felt the heat rising in her cheeks. She had been staring at the man like a frightened parlour maid who had just been discovered standing over a shattered piece of porcelain. Yet she had never been in such a position before, and it was hardly surprising if she found it difficult to approach a subject as troubling as it was urgent.

'Mr Rodrigo,' she began slowly, 'although we have met only briefly in the past, I know that you have had business dealings with my father on several occasions. I believe that you have advanced him money . . .'

He frowned. 'Are you here on your father's business?'

'No indeed.' She shook her head in emphatic denial. 'I merely hoped that your acquaintance with him would lead you to look more kindly upon my request.'

'My dear Miss Halliwell,' the man before her said warmly, 'you have no need of recommendation from anyone. You may be assured of my aid, whatever you may ask.'

She held her breath for a moment, for the intensity of his gaze was more than mere kindness. She had occasionally entertained the fancy that Mr Rodrigo's interest in her might be more than mere friendship. Now she could hardly dismiss this very real possibility. Still, she had come too far to draw back now.

'I am of a mind to open a small milliner's shop,' she blurted out in a rush. 'Nothing too grand, mind you — but I would need financial assistance to begin with. I would keep the strictest account of any money advanced to me, and you would be paid back every penny with interest.'

It was clear that he had not anticipated this. For a moment his face was quite blank. Then his dark brows drew together as he considered the matter.

'You wish to open a shop here in Bath?'

'No, no,' she hastened to explain. 'In Bristol, perhaps — or possibly Southampton.'

'It is a most unusual ambition for a young lady of your rank,' he said slowly, his look far too piercing and perceptive. 'I cannot help but wonder what has inspired it?'

'My reasons are personal, sir.' She hoped that she did not sound ungrateful and began to see that there might be no alternative to full disclosure.

He rose from his seat and made his way around the desk to stand beside her.

'If you have had a — disagreement — with your father, I advise you to do nothing rash which you may regret later.'

'We are destitute, sir,' Anthea said bluntly. The time for reticence was clearly past.

'My dear!' His look of compassion was more dreadful than any questioning might be. 'Perhaps I may be able to assist your father . . .'

'You would be foolish to do so, sir,' she answered briskly, giving him a direct look. 'Papa would certainly lose it all at the gaming tables.'

'It cannot be as bad as you believe,' he suggested optimistically. 'A little economy, a more judicious use of Sir Harry's assets . . .'

'Assets!' Anthea interrupted with a hollow laugh. 'I wish you luck in finding any.'

Mr Rodrigo compressed his lips in silence. Having dealt with her feckless parent on several occasions, he no doubt concluded that she might well have the right of it in her assessment of the situation.

'So will you help me, sir?' she asked again, squaring her shoulders.

'I do not like to think of you eking out an existence by such paltry means, Miss Halliwell. There must be an alternative.'

'Yes,' she agreed miserably. 'My father has graciously consented to allow me to move with him to Avon Street, to share the home of Mrs Pomfrit.'

'Avon Street!' Rodrigo exclaimed, plainly appalled. He could not but be aware that this address was more famed for pickpockets and Paphians than for genteel accommodations. 'I cannot allow that,' he concluded with finality.

'Then you will advance me the money?' She breathed a sigh of relief.

'No.'

'So,' she swallowed the lump of fear and defeat which rose to her throat, 'for all your assurances, you are unwilling to offer me aid?' She stood up, trying to recover what tattered dignity remained to her. 'Forgive me for having taken up your time, sir.'

'If you will hear me out, Miss Halliwell,' he answered, stepping forward to block her hasty exit, 'I would offer you another solution to your dilemma.'

* * *

At this interesting moment, Mrs Norton arrived with the tea tray, regarding them both suspiciously before retreating at a sign from her employer. The small diversion was a welcome respite for Anthea. This was not an interview which anyone could find enjoyable. In spite of the trappings of elegance and politeness, she was essentially a beggar in need of whatever crumbs she might contrive to acquire.

Rodrigo carefully performed the office of pouring tea while his guest used the time to calm herself. She took a sip, reviving her spirits momentarily, and eyed him above the rim of her cup.

'You were saying, sir?' she inquired, as the silence between them stretched rather longer than she found tolerable.

'You have met my daughter, Miss Halliwell.' Anthea blinked at him, unable to discern any possible connection between his offspring and her own dilemma. 'Rachel is a precocious girl who needs a woman's guidance in matters which I, as a mere man, am not suited to instruct her.'

'Your daughter is surely too old to need a governess, sir. Are you seeking a paid companion?' Anthea was not certain whether such employment would be preferable to that of a milliner, but she was hardly in a position to decline any reasonable offer.

'I am desirous of bringing Rachel out into Bath society.' He paused significantly. 'As you may imagine, my knowledge of such matters is limited. Had her mother been alive, of course, it would have been a different matter.'

'I do not see how I would be of any use to you, sir,' Anthea replied flatly. 'It would hardly be appropriate for me, as your daughter's companion, to take charge of such social events as would necessarily have to be arranged.'

'As her companion, no,' he agreed coolly. 'But as my wife, nothing would be more natural.'

Anthea almost let fall her teacup but managed to hold on before it deposited its contents in her lap. Surely she could not have heard him correctly!

'I beg your pardon, sir?'

'You must be surprised,' he acknowledged — which she considered a gross understatement. 'I confess that the notion has only just occurred to me.'

'Has it?' she asked faintly.

'Yes.' He sat down in the matching chair which was placed before the desk at a slight angle to her own. 'I have been quite at a loss as to how I would manage Rachel's presentation in a creditable manner. It seems to me, however, that this is a solution which would settle both our difficulties at once.'

'But I — you — we . . .' Anthea found herself babbling incoherently.

'I understand your reservations, my dear,' the gentleman said gently. 'We are scarcely acquainted, and you certainly have had no time to consider the matter. If my offer is entirely repugnant to you, then you have every right to refuse it.'

'Oh no!' she cried, not wishing him to think that she considered him at all beneath her touch. 'But it is so . . . unexpected.'

'You need not fear any ill-usage in my house, Miss Halliwell. I have the greatest respect and esteem for you.' He reached across to take her left hand briefly in his. 'You would have no more material worries either. You shall not find me ungenerous.'

'I—I have no fears on that head,' she stammered, startled by the tingling sensation at the touch of his hand.

'What then?' he asked. 'Have you another attachment, perhaps? Is there a gentleman from whom you expect an offer?'

'Hardly, sir.' The idea was ludicrous, as he must know.

'Then I ask you to give the matter your consideration.' He released her hand. 'Perhaps your independence is dearer to you, but I offer you a home where your comfort and happiness would always be considered, and where you would want for nothing that money can procure. Your future would be secure and your needs and wants attended to. Forgive me,' he continued a little diffidently, 'but would that not be preferable to the precarious and uncertain future which must be yours if you pursue the course you have described to me?'

She could not deny that the picture which he painted was a very pleasant one. She did not consider herself mercenary, but it was impossible not to be tempted by the carrot he dangled so enticingly before her. Life in King Street had been anything but easy, and she had to admit that she did not relish the thought of earning her living in a profession which might well prove to be unsuccessful. She had proposed it only because she could see no reasonable alternative. But now that he had offered her a chance of wealth and security beyond anything she had ever anticipated, did she dare refuse him? Marriage was indeed a drastic step but many had taken it on far less promising grounds.

'I do not know what to say,' she answered at length, with perfect truth.

'Then say nothing for the moment,' he advised sensibly. 'Return to your home and give yourself time to dwell more fully on the matter.'

There was one thing more, however, which she must lay before him. She stood rather shakily, and he immediately followed suit. Only three feet of space now separated them, and she forced herself to look him fully in the face. Drawing a deep breath, she nerved herself to say what she desperately longed to avoid saying.

'I think that there is something you should know, sir, before you proceed with this.'

'Yes, Miss Halliwell?'

'You may well wish to withdraw your offer when you learn that the woman whom you have just asked to become your wife is generally held to be a common thief.'

CHAPTER TWO: MARRY IN HASTE

In the silence which followed this pronouncement, Anthea waited stiffly for the blow to fall. She looked him in the eyes, nerving herself against the shock and disgust which they might display.

'I am aware,' he said gently, never flinching, 'of the scandal which has caused you such undeserved suffering.'

'What!' There seemed to be no end of the surprises this man had in store for her. 'You know of this, and still you wish to marry me?'

'My dear, it is common knowledge in this city but I see no reason why it should be an impediment to our union,' he said, quite matter-of-fact. 'Nothing would ever convince me that you are guilty of the crime of which you are suspected.'

'But you cannot be certain that I am innocent!' she exclaimed, more shocked by this than by anything that had gone before.

'Unless you yourself should swear otherwise to me,' he told her, his dark eyes inexplicably kind, 'then I am as certain of your innocence as I have ever been of anything.'

This was the most incredible development of all. That this man — a virtual stranger — should have such unwavering faith in her. She caught her lips between her milk-white teeth, willing the tears back into her eyes. It had been so long since anyone had looked upon her without suspicion that she could scarcely credit anything so beautiful. Her own father had never been entirely convinced that she had not purloined Georgina's necklace.

'I was never formally charged . . .' she began, feeling she must speak before she disgraced herself by weeping.

'I know.' He placed a strong, lean hand upon her shoulder — a familiar gesture which should have been impertinent but was oddly comforting. 'It would almost have been better to have had your day in court. Rumour and innuendo can be more damning than outright prosecution.'

She looked at him in wonder. He truly did seem to comprehend her situation. Nobody else had ever entered into what she had felt these past seven years.

'Had I been put on trial, I would probably have been hanged — or at present residing in Australia.' She shook her head. 'The evidence against me was overwhelming. I cannot blame anyone for doubting my veracity.'

'*I* would never doubt it,' he said simply.

'How did you learn of this?'

'Although I came to Bath more than a year after the incident, it was not long before I heard the whole story. It is common knowledge.' He removed his hand to make a dismissive gesture. 'The details were related to me by Mr Feingold, the jeweller involved in the case.'

'And did he think me guilty?'

'He did.'

'Yet you would take my word over his?'

'I would not be inclined to doubt anything you told me.'

'Why?' She was mystified.

He gave a self-deprecating shrug. 'Let us say that I pride myself upon being a fairly astute judge of character.'

'I am most truly grateful for your confidence.' This was the literal truth, at least.

'If you would express your gratitude,' he said with a smile, 'go home to New King Street and think seriously on my proposal.'

'There is no need to do so.' She drew a deep breath and plunged in without further hesitation. 'I will marry you, sir.'

* * *

Anthea barely had time to close Gideon Rodrigo's front door behind her before Miss Rodrigo descended upon her father's study.

'Am I to wish you joy, Papa?' she demanded at once, mincing no words.

'What on earth do you mean, Rachel?' he asked.

'Are you, or are you not, going to marry Miss Halliwell?'

'Were you listening at the door?' He was quite put out.

'No I was not,' she corrected him. 'I was watching from the bend in the stairs, until she left.'

'Really, Rachel! And what made you think that I am marrying Miss Halliwell?'

'Well, it's perfectly obvious that you are in love with her,' his amazing daughter announced.

Gideon could feel his cheeks grow warmer, despite his best efforts.

'Why should you think so?' he snapped.

'If you had seen your face when I announced her earlier, you would not ask such a silly question.'

He seated himself once more at his desk, rested his left elbow on the top and leaned his forehead upon his hand.

'What am I to do with you, you impertinent chit?'

'Perhaps my new stepmother will be able to curb my tongue,' she suggested cheekily.

'I doubt it,' he muttered.

'So you *are* going to marry her!' She dropped into the chair recently vacated by Anthea. 'I never knew you were such a dark horse, Papa — fostering a secret passion for a perfectly unsuitable young woman.'

'I have been doing no such thing,' he contradicted her, with more volume than truth.

'Oh, I do not blame you in the least,' Rachel answered airily. 'She is positively a diamond of the first water — and you do have an eye for gems, after all.'

'This,' he said with slow deliberation, 'is a marriage of convenience.'

She gave a laugh of utter incredulity. 'It is certainly convenient for *her* to marry a man of wealth and some consequence — even if he bears the stain of being Jewish. The only thing you can possibly get out of it is the lady herself. But I begin to suspect that is what you have wanted all along.'

'And if I have?' Now he was becoming defensive, somewhat annoyed that his daughter was so easily able to decipher his emotions. He hoped that Anthea was not so perspicacious.

'I wish you every happiness, Papa.' She was suddenly serious. 'If anyone deserves happiness, it is you. I know your marriage to Mama was not of your choosing, and that you were never suited. Somehow, I believe that Miss Halliwell will indeed give you what until now you have been denied.'

'I have been tail-over-top in love with her from the first moment I met her,' he confessed at last. 'But I feel quite ashamed at having used her current situation to my own advantage in this way. I am behaving like a selfish swine, with no thought of her own feelings.'

'Nonsense.' His dutiful daughter dismissed this with a careless shrug. 'It is every woman's dream to have a husband who can not only provide every material comfort but the passion which I do not doubt she has been sadly lacking. She's a fool if she does not realize how truly fortunate she is — and Miss Halliwell strikes me as a very intelligent woman.'

'I hope that you are right, my dear.'

'I expect to have a baby brother within a year,' Rachel prophesied, at which her father lowered his head into both hands, deciding that he had even greater need of Anthea than even he had realized.

CHAPTER THREE: A FUGITIVE FROM HOME

The short walk to her father's residence was accomplished in such a daze that Anthea was unaware of how she got there or whether she had passed anyone else on the street. She managed to slip into the house without being seen and sought the sanctuary of her bedchamber, while trying to come to terms with all that had happened on this momentous afternoon.

She was going to marry Gideon Rodrigo! With one simple 'yes' all her immediate problems would be solved. Marriage to a Jew was frowned on by persons of the first respectability. But his large fortune would undoubtedly cover a multitude of social sins in the eyes of many. He was, after all, every inch the gentleman. There was a difference in age, perhaps — but not so great as to be a real impediment, especially to a female in her position: a woman of seven-and-twenty who was now considered to be 'on the shelf' and whose charms and beauty would only continue to decline with each new spring.

What really determined her to accept his offer, however, was the one thing more fantastic than anything she had imagined possible: his absolute faith in her. He said he had no doubts at all that she had been unjustly accused and her character was blameless. For that alone, she felt that she would be a perfect ninnyhammer to refuse him.

Eventually she fell into a comfortable doze, from which she was awakened several hours later by a knock upon her door which heralded the intrusion of the maid, Pamela, with the news that Sir Harry had returned. Anthea applied herself to the task of making herself presentable so that she might face her father with the news of her decision.

* * *

Descending from her room, she found her father settled comfortably into a large armchair in the parlour. He had been a handsome man in his youth, though years of reckless self-indulgence had long ago begun to chip away at his once finely chiselled countenance. After a pleasant afternoon with Mrs Pomfrit, he was in an agreeable mood, unaware of the fate which was about to befall him.

He greeted his daughter with a slight grunt, not bothering to rise, and she wondered if he noticed her dowdy green gown — another done-over remnant of her youthful wardrobe, once lovely and fashionable, now worn and faded.

'Good evening, Papa,' she said.

'What is it, girl?' he snapped, irritated with her as usual.

'I wish to inform you that I will not be accompanying you to Avon Street,' she announced, wasting no time.

'What do you mean?' He frowned. 'If you mean to remain here, I'd like to know how you'll afford it!'

'I shall not stay in New King Street,' she answered calmly. 'After my marriage, I will be residing in Charles Street.'

'Marriage!' He stared at her for a moment before being overtaken by a fit of convulsive laughter, the tears rolling down his reddened cheeks. 'You're all about in the head, girl.'

'Nevertheless, I am going to marry Gideon Rodrigo.'

'You and the Jew!' His eyes narrowed as he suddenly sobered. 'What nonsense is this?'

'Mr Rodrigo has offered for me and I have accepted him.'

17

'I don't know if you're bamming me but if not then I'll tell you this: I'll not have it! No daughter of mine will disgrace my name by allying herself with that Crucifier.'

'This sudden attack of religious fervour is quite out of place, Papa,' his unrepentant daughter told him. 'Mr Rodrigo is a baptized Christian who attends St Swithin's — a fact with which you might be acquainted, did you ever grace that building with your presence.'

'Once a Jew, always a Jew,' was his reply.

'Well, he will soon be your son-in-law.'

'I utterly forbid it!' he pronounced awfully.

'You cannot,' she said without flinching. 'I am past the age where your consent is necessary, sir. I was merely informing you of the fact.'

'I'll see you in Hell rather!' he shouted wildly, almost standing up in his anger.

'You will be there soon enough, no doubt.' She looked him directly in the eye. 'It is highly unlikely that any other offer will ever be made to me, in my situation. I am fortunate to have received this one and am not likely to refuse it in order to satisfy your misplaced pride.'

He subsided into his chair once more, looking balefully at her.

'I will not be able to hold up my head in polite society,' he countered.

'You can scarcely do so now,' she pointed out, adding, 'You have often expressed your concern that you would be saddled with an ape-leader for the rest of your life. Now that grim fate can be avoided. You should be grateful to a gentleman like Mr Rodrigo.'

'Gentleman!' he snorted his contempt. 'A heathen merchant, his hands tainted with ill-gotten gains.'

'Must you speak like something out of a Gothic novel?' she asked wearily.

'If you wed Rodrigo, you are no longer my daughter.'

'So be it.'

This careless attitude was too much for him. The cup of his wrath was now full and overflowed upon her.

'If you are determined on this, then I wash my hands of you! I suggest that you leave this house tonight and never darken my door again.'

As he spoke, he rose and stepped forward, ending his oration by seizing her upper arm and thrusting her out of the room with such force that she fell against the wall opposite and only just managed to prevent herself from sinking to the floor.

'Very well, sir.' Her anger now almost matched his own. 'You shall have your wish. Goodbye, Papa. And may God have more pity on you than you have shown to your own flesh and blood.'

* * *

In less than an hour, Anthea was trudging along the pavement in Charles Street for the second time that day. She carried two battered bandboxes in her hand, the pitiful sum of her worldly goods — or as many as she counted worth taking with her.

It was almost dark now, and she felt a sudden chill which was not entirely due to the cool evening air. Earlier today she had feared for her future, wondering what she would do if Gideon Rodrigo refused to lend her aid. Now that she had accepted his unexpected offer, she was aware of a new fear. What was to become of her? What would it be like to be the wife of such a man? She did not worry about what people would say: too much had already been said about her over the years for her to mind such things anymore. But why did she feel such a strange mixture of apprehension and excitement? Why did her pulse race each time she encountered Rodrigo's gaze, and her head feel so dizzy when he touched her?

Should she turn and run away? Was the handsome Jew a knight in shining armour, or the Devil in disguise? Was she mad even to contemplate the desperate step she was taking?

Her mind went round and round, but still she moved steadily closer to his house until she stood before the door once more. For the second time that day, she knocked for admittance and was greeted by the stern-faced Mrs Norton.

'May I come in?' she inquired, as if she were there for afternoon tea.

'I think you'd better, miss,' the housekeeper answered, opening the door wider and eyeing her with a little more compassion than she had shown earlier.

CHAPTER FOUR: SCANDAL-BROTH SUPPER

Gideon Rodrigo was sitting down to dinner with his daughter when a pronounced knock at his front door caused him to turn his head in surprise. They certainly were not expecting any visitors tonight.

'Who on earth can that be, Papa?' Rachel wondered aloud.

'Someone on urgent business, one would assume.'

The murmur of voices in the hallway could be heard through the open door of the dining room and was followed by the tread of footsteps headed in their general direction. A moment later, Mrs Norton appeared in the doorway.

'It's the young lady who was here earlier, sir,' she said, barely concealing her disapproval of such goings-on in what had before been a most respectable household.

'Good heavens! Show Miss Halliwell in at once.'

In less than a minute the young lady in question tumbled into the room, her attire somewhat dishevelled and clutching a battered bandbox in each hand.

'My dear!' Gideon advanced quickly to her. 'Whatever has happened?'

'My father has banished me from his house, sir,' she answered simply. 'I came directly here.' She swallowed. 'I had nowhere else to go.'

'Where else should you go?' He was eager to put her as much at ease as was possible in such fantastic circumstances. 'Indeed, this is now your home, Anthea.'

'Thank you, sir,' she almost choked, whether in gratitude or embarrassment he could not tell.

'You know my daughter, Rachel.'

Anthea smiled and bowed awkwardly, while Gideon led her to the table and seated her at a chair beside him.

'Have you had your dinner, ma'am?' Rachel asked, looking at her as though she expected her to faint at any moment.

Anthea confessed that she had not eaten properly since breakfast.

'You must be quite starved,' Rachel said, her eyes taking in the other woman's worn muslin gown which had once been white but had over time faded into a dull cream colour.

'Your father,' Gideon remarked, turning the conversation, 'did not take kindly to the prospect of your marrying a Jew?'

Anthea blushed and looked away in some discomfort but made no attempt to disguise the truth.

'He did not,' she agreed, then raised her chin and gave him a direct look. 'However, I informed him that he no longer had any authority to prevent it, and that I would do as I pleased.'

'Then it is settled.' He nodded decisively.

'So long,' Anthea said, with a glance at Rachel, 'as your daughter is not opposed to the match.'

'I?' Rachel looked quite taken aback. 'It's hardly my place to object to my father's choice of bride.'

'You are willing to overlook my deplorable wardrobe?' she quizzed, with a fugitive smile.

'I know that you are quizzing me,' the young lady retorted. 'But I respect my father's opinion in such matters, and I believe that you and I shall get along famously together, in spite of the general portrayal of stepmothers in fashionable literature.'

'I suspect that I shall quite enjoy having you for a step-daughter,' Anthea said, and meant it. Rachel was an impishly engaging young lady.

'And we will doubtless be able to do something about your wardrobe — with all possible speed!'

Anthea's lips twitched, and Gideon could not forbear a chuckle.

'As you see, my dear,' he told her, 'your task is likely to be a difficult one.'

'What task?' his daughter asked suspiciously.

'Never mind,' he replied, concentrating on Anthea.

'So what are you going to do now?'

'I think we must be married at once.'

'At once!' his two listeners echoed in unison.

'We shall elope tonight.'

Gideon seemed quite unruffled at the prospect of an act which was what persons of gentility frowned upon. But, as he pointed out practically, there was little choice. Anthea could not remain under his roof for any length of time without creating even greater scandal. In the interim, if they waited for the banns to be called, she had no relations with whom she could seek shelter. It was best to 'cut the Gordian knot' and get leg-shackled at once. If they left for London tonight, they would be there before noon on the morrow. A Special License might then be obtained and they could be married within a day or two.

'We shall spend a fortnight with my friends, the Guzmans, at Richmond Hill,' he concluded. 'By the time we return to Bath, the whole affair will be an accomplished fact — which should spare us the worst stares and whispers.'

'I hope so,' Anthea answered doubtfully.

'You must see to packing a trunk, Rachel,' Gideon told his daughter. 'I will have my man do the same for me.'

'That will not do at all.' Rachel was strongly opposed.

'What do you mean?'

'Only a complete gudgeon carries his daughter with him when eloping!'

'You seem to be quite conversant with the proper etiquette in such situations,' he quipped.

23

'It is not at all the thing,' she assured him. 'A favourite pet may be allowed on such occasions but a child is most inappropriate.'

'But this is no ordinary elopement,' Anthea responded, feeling that the situation was becoming more fantastic by the minute. 'We are not a romantic young couple, after all.'

'Nonsense!' Rachel would not be dissuaded. 'Nothing could be more romantic.'

'If you like, then,' Gideon suggested, apparently accepting her premise, 'I shall ask Cousin Rhoda to stay with you while we are on our . . . our wedding trip.'

'Excellent!' she agreed. 'She leads a very dull life with her mama in Queen Square and will be glad to escape for a fortnight or so.'

Mrs Norton chose that moment to enter, followed by a maid. They served the simple meal, which was actually very well prepared and filling, but tasted remarkably like sawdust to Anthea. When it was over, and Mrs Norton was about to make a dignified exit, Gideon halted her.

'Mrs Norton, will you kindly send Liggett to me at once. I shall be eloping with Miss Halliwell this evening and must contrive to hire a carriage.'

Had she been struck by lightning, Mrs Norton could not have looked more thoroughly amazed. Her mouth fell open in such comic surprise that the trio watching was hard-pressed to keep from going into whoops.

'I beg your pardon, sir?' she stammered at last, convinced that she had not heard correctly.

Gideon repeated his request, and the poor housekeeper staggered from the room to fulfil the most incredible request her employer had ever made.

* * *

All was arranged with positively indecent haste and much scurrying to and fro by Mr Rodrigo's servants. Every moment brought some new impropriety, pushing Anthea toward a fate which was now all but inescapable.

Could she possibly be doing such a thing? Was there even now another way out of her situation? But there was hardly time to think. One minute she was trying to ignore Mrs Norton's disapproving stare — the next she was smiling at Rachel's lamentations that she was too short to lend Anthea a decent gown. Meanwhile, she watched Gideon as he calmly arranged all with near-military precision.

Just before midnight they climbed into the hired coach which Liggett, Gideon's much-harassed valet, had managed to procure as if by magic. Then they waved goodbye as the conveyance made its way through the well-lit streets of Bath, heading for the London Road. As they drew away from the city, Anthea was seized by a sudden, overwhelming weariness. Much to her own surprise, she fell asleep almost at once.

CHAPTER FIVE: NO TURNING BACK

She awoke with a start, feeling completely disorientated and utterly unable to recall where she was. Then, as consciousness returned gradually, she became aware that her head was resting on a broad shoulder and the warmth around her was the arm of Gideon Rodrigo.

'Oh!' she exclaimed in some confusion. 'Please forgive me, sir.'

'Gideon,' he corrected, smiling at her. 'Under the circumstances, it will not do to be so formal, my dear. And I assure you I am perfectly content with my situation.'

She stared at him as if he had transformed into a serpent. What was she doing? What had she done? She had eloped with Gideon Rodrigo. That was all.

'I had not intended to fall asleep,' she answered stupidly.

His smile broadened but he only said, 'Will you tell me something about yourself, Anthea? We know so little of one another. Do you not think it time we became better acquainted?'

She could not argue with this and began to tell him of the happier period of her life, before the family moved to Bath.

'My father brought my mother here to take the waters for her health.' She frowned, remembering. 'She had never had a strong constitution, however, and it was all to no avail. In spite of everything that the Pump Room and the Queen's Bath could offer, and the efforts of Dr Bowen, my mother died within a year of our quitting Derbyshire.'

Like a flock of singing birds released from an aviary, a host of memories crowded Anthea's mind. She found herself recounting far more than she had intended. She recalled that her parents had seemed quite happy together. It was only after Mama's death, when Anthea was a girl of fourteen, that her father began to drink and gamble to excess, spinning ever downward until he had reached the nadir he boasted of today. They had moved several times over the years: first to St James's Square, then to Gay Street, and finally to New King Street. What depths her father might yet sink to she hardly dared to ponder. Avoiding any details concerning the unfortunate affair in her past, she concluded her narrative.

'And what of you, Gideon?' she asked at length, realizing that they had covered several miles during her recital. He settled back in his seat.

'My father,' he told her, 'was a successful stockbroker in London. He built a house in Finsbury Square, though I have now removed to Mayfair.'

'Did your father convert?' she could not resist inquiring.

'No.' He shrugged. 'Though he had more than his share of quarrels with Bevis Marks, he never abandoned the religion to which he was born.'

'Bevis Marks?'

'The great synagogue in London,' he elucidated.

'And you?'

'I was something of a rebel, I suppose.' He chuckled softly to himself.

'I find that difficult to believe.'

'Oh, I was a dutiful son,' he hastened to assure her, 'but I had my own ideas. I associated with Christians — as many young sons of well-to-do Jewish families do — and I began to question the received wisdom of the Talmud and the rabbis. I secretly read the New Testament and became convinced of its truth. I was baptized into the Church of England of my own accord, which produced an irrevocable break with my father.'

'And your wife?' she ventured, hoping that she did not seem over-bold.

'Hannah?' He paused for a moment, frowning as if at an unpleasant memory. 'She was chosen for me by my father, as is often the case in the old Jewish families. It was not a happy union.'

He married at twenty and was widowed within ten years. He had done his duty but never truly loved his wife, nor had she had much in common with him. She wondered if he had ever looked outside of the marriage for the pleasures he did not find within it, then chided herself for such intimate and ungenerous thoughts. With her father as her nearest example, however, perhaps they were natural enough.

Gideon had moved to Bath because he considered it a better place to establish himself and to rear his young daughter. It was a town of somewhat faded respectability where an enterprising man of fortune might penetrate the ranks of the gentry and lesser nobility with relative ease. No doubt his marriage to the daughter of a baronet — albeit a profligate and impoverished one — was a step higher on the ladder to social advancement.

She knew more about him now than at any time in the five years since he had come to town. She had seen him briefly whenever he visited the house to consult with her father. Most of her mother's jewellery had no doubt passed through this man's hands at some point, and she felt a momentary revulsion that he had assisted — however unwittingly — in helping to take even such small memories from her. But he was a man of business, not a plaster saint, and was far less to blame than her father, who had not hesitated to rob his own daughter of her rightful inheritance.

On the whole, she had always been impressed by Gideon Rodrigo. Though they had met perhaps half a dozen times, and spoken only the most perfunctory greetings, there was something about him which had drawn her to him from the outset, and she had never really considered applying for help to anyone else.

* * *

As for Gideon, he was every bit as unsettled as his bride. What would she say, he wondered, if she knew that the man who had proposed to her yesterday was a fraud? While it was true that he was eager to help her out of her present difficulties, his motives were not quite as pure as that. For all his chivalrous instincts, there was a current of desire behind it that he had never been able to deny.

That Anthea, born a gentleman's daughter with every advantage, should be reduced to keeping a shop and living in pitiful lodgings, was simply unbearable. He could not allow it. But he was honest enough to admit — at least to himself — that it was his own passion for her which prompted him to press ahead with his offer of marriage before reason could squash so preposterous a scheme. He had seen her look of surprise — even shock. But she had not completely recoiled from it.

Now, for the very first time, he began to hope. He did not dare to suppose that she could ever actually love him. For her this marriage was a matter of necessity rather than inclination. But by some mysterious twist of fate, the woman he had wanted for so long was about to become his wife. It was far more than he could have imagined four and twenty hours before. For now, it was enough that she was with him. How long he could keep his passions in check, he did not know. He might not have been born a gentleman but he must strive to behave like one!

But even as he began to adjust his thoughts to the unexpected developments of the day, his mind was moving forward and slowly but steadily forming a new scheme. For he was well aware that, while this marriage would solve Anthea's pecuniary problems and free her from the tyranny of total dependence upon her father, there was that other matter of which they had barely spoken.

Unfortunately, he could not undo the damage that gossip and speculation had done to her reputation, the shadow of suspicion that would always cripple her socially. She had been effectively ostracized from polite society, and her marriage to a Jew would hardly be of benefit in improving her position. While his own friends might accept her, the class into which she had been born still considered her to be someone with whom they could not associate. Former acquaintances would still distance themselves from her. Old harridans like a Lady Drummond or a Mrs Leigh Perrot would never accept her, although that particular lady was hardly a paragon and had been as close as made no difference to hanging for theft! But she had been given her day in court and had triumphed. She could hold her head high and stick her nose firmly into the air — which it was impossible for Anthea to do. It was no secret that Mr Sheridan himself had eloped with the daughter of the celebrated Lindley family of Bath. It was not an unprecedented act, by any means. But neither was it what respectable families would boast of.

For himself, Gideon did not care what anyone thought. He loved her and nothing could ever convince him of her guilt. But it must be a festering sore to her and a source of endless shame and embarrassment, to put it no higher. It must not be allowed to continue.

Everyone, he thought, was possessed of some talent — some gift given by their Creator to be used for their own betterment and the benefit of mankind. His father had been a brilliant man of business, and Gideon considered himself to be particularly skilled in the knowledge and cutting of gemstones, among other things. However, what he needed now was someone with a different kind of talent. If Anthea was ever to be delivered from the social purgatory into which she had been forced, it demanded extraordinary abilities possessed by relatively few.

Fortunately, through his acquaintance with a certain Frenchman, he had become aware of just such a person — or rather, two persons. He had never met these remarkable individuals but he was certain that they were exactly what he required. Whether he could persuade them to lend him their aid was another question altogether. He rather fancied that they might well be intrigued by his request.

Well, he would not permit them to refuse him! Failure was not an option. For Anthea's sake he must succeed.

CHAPTER SIX: THE MARRIAGE OF TRUE MINDS

It was twilight when they drew up before the large residence of the Guzmans somewhere in the neighbourhood of Twickenham. Gideon had assured her that these friends of his would be happy to offer her a temporary home while arrangements were made for their wedding. He stepped down from the carriage, instructing Anthea to remain within. She drew back into the shadows, glancing rather apprehensively through the window while he entered the front door of the house. Not many minutes passed before the door was opened once more and an amazing figure burst forth from it.

Mrs Lavinia Guzman, plump and pretty in a faded way, was dressed in an evening gown the shade of a Seville orange. Its simple lines, however, were almost obscured by the addition of multiple frilled flounces and bows. She hopped down the steps like a brightly plumed bird, talking as she came.

'My dear Miss Halliwell,' she twittered, opening the carriage door herself and squeezing her head and shoulders in to take Anthea's hand in a crushing but genial grip, 'what a brute Gideon is to keep you kicking your heels outside. Come in, come in, I beg you.'

Caught between laughter and gratitude, Anthea tried to express her thanks but was scarcely allowed a word. Lavinia practically hauled her out of the conveyance and marched her up the stairs.

'Here is my husband,' she announced, indicating an equally stout gentleman in his early forties who stood beaming beside Gideon.

Mr Guzman attempted to introduce himself but was forestalled by his wife.

'Wiggins!' she shouted over his more subdued tones, 'prepare the best guest room for the young lady. Be quick about it now!'

Once within the house, her hostess was even more overwhelming than she had seemed in the evening shadows. She was decked out in a positive blaze of jewels — emeralds and diamonds of enormous size at her wrist and throat, with matching jewels dangling from her ears. An intricately fashioned brooch of pearls and garnets clung precariously to the scant bit of silk which barely covered her prominent bosom. Her hair, arranged in what appeared to be a thousand bobbing ringlets, was topped by yet more diamonds in the form of an elaborate tiara.

At first Anthea supposed that they must be on their way to a ball or reception of some kind but soon learned that the couple was dining quite alone. She could not help but conjecture what the lady might wear on a more formal occasion. Nothing could be a greater contrast to her own faded and outmoded attire, and she wondered which of them was more picturesque.

'It is too, too thrilling!' Lavinia was babbling happily. 'I have always dreamed of assisting in an elopement but such an opportunity has never before presented itself.'

'We are happy to assist you in achieving your ambition, my dear Lavinia,' Gideon declared. Anthea caught the gleam in his eye, which nearly overset her determined gravity.

'You are always so kind, Gideon.' The affection in her voice was clearly genuine. 'But I must confess that I never expected you to do anything so dashing as to spirit a young lady away like this.'

'I am almost as surprised as you are,' Gideon confessed.

Mrs Guzman next herded them gently but firmly into a large drawing room decorated in the very latest style. With its preponderance of carving and gilding, it was too ornate for Anthea's taste, but it was clear that no expense had been spared in the furnishings.

'Are you madly, desperately in love with each other?' she demanded, clasping her hands together in vicarious rapture as she gazed upon the unlikely couple.

'But of course,' Gideon replied promptly. 'What other explanation could there be?'

Anthea knew not which way to look or what to say. She had not expected the man to possess such a wicked sense of humour. Almost every word was tempting her to laugh.

'One can hardly wonder at you being smitten with this young lady,' their host said gallantly. 'She is a veritable diamond, Gideon.'

'Divinely beautiful!' his wife concurred, while Anthea blushed uncomfortably.

'I charge you both to take the greatest care of her while I am in town,' Gideon admonished them.

'I am to remain here, then?'

'Do not worry, child,' Lavinia reassured her. 'I am sure he will not be parted from you for one moment longer than is necessary.'

'Everything should be well in train in a day or two.'

* * *

Anthea felt strangely abandoned upon Gideon's departure. While he was with her, she felt secure and unafraid. Now that she was left alone with strangers, doubts began to assail her on every side.

Lavinia gave her little time to dwell on such matters. Her dressmaker, Madame Fleuride (formerly Betty Gutchins of Liverpool) was summoned the very next day. If the modiste objected to such high-handed treatment, she did not betray as much. Mrs Guzman was her wealthiest and most lucrative client, and money was money.

The three ladies spent several hours happily poring over sketches of willowy goddesses in the pages of *La Belle Assemblée*, discussing the various merits of muslins, silks and taffetas. Anthea was subjected to being measured, poked and prodded while Madame exclaimed over the gracefulness of her form. Her own long-neglected interest in fashion began to revive under such flattering attention. She could see that the little woman had a genuine gift and was very much attuned to the needs of her clientele. It may have been that she was inspired by the challenge of transforming an ugly duckling into a swan. In any case, with Anthea's approval, she diplomatically dismissed several of Lavinia's more outrageous suggestions and eagerly adopted the simplicity of Anthea's choices.

Madame promised to ruthlessly sacrifice a gown which she had been making for a lady who was really too ancient to wear it as it should be worn. It would be altered that very evening. In the meantime, she would fashion an afternoon gown of fine muslin, over which might be worn a cherry-red pelisse she had put by until she could find a customer worthy of it. Now, she asserted, that customer had arrived. One or two other gowns would be ready before Anthea returned to Bath. It was at least the foundation of a real wardrobe, and Madame hoped that the new Mrs Rodrigo would remember her in future.

It was the kind of pleasure Anthea had not known since the giddy days of her first season. Papa had been rather plump in the pockets then, and she had worn the latest fashions. It was pleasant to once again command such attention, yet very strange as well.

Anthea finally escaped the confines of the house to take a leisurely stroll through the grounds. The park, though not large, was quite delightful. It had been a long time since she had set foot in anything larger than the small, enclosed garden at the back of the house in New King Street, and the idyllic beauty around her seemed to bathe her soul in quiet tranquillity. A wide expanse of lawn sloped down toward the Thames, which weaved its way gently through banks dotted with nodding trees of beech and willow, curving away in the distance like a silver-gilt high road.

The very air was thick with the scent of exhilaration — of new-found freedom. It seemed to her that the world was opening up, offering her a new life. Yet what did the future truly hold? What would it be like to be married to Gideon Rodrigo? She seated herself on a nearby bench for a few moments, pondering this question. He seemed kind and generous but would she not be exchanging one prison for another? It might be a gilded prison, perhaps, but still it was not entirely of her choosing. Or was it? She shook her head, disturbed by the sudden and unexpected sensation of antic-ipation as she thought of Gideon becoming her husband. Why was the thought so pleasant to her?

A wood pigeon rose from a nearby thicket, distracting her momentarily. She sighed and stood once more, turning her back on the river and making her way towards the house. Whatever her feelings might be, her choice was made.

* * *

While Anthea was trying to come to terms with her situation, Gideon was not idle. He made arrangements with the staff at his London house, preparing them for the arrival of a new mis-tress in due time. He also attended to his business and visited those members of his family who had not completely disowned him. They were pleasantly scandalized at the news of his elope-ment with a beautiful young lady, even if she was a Christian.

Finally, after much thought and consideration, Gideon sat down at his desk on the evening before his wedding day and began to write a letter, to be delivered to a small village in Sussex:

Dear Mr Savidge, it began, *I hope that you will forgive this somewhat unusual request from a total stranger.*

CHAPTER SEVEN: A LITTLE DIVERSION

'Lydia,' Mr John Savidge said to his wife, 'how would you like to spend a few weeks in Bath?'

'Bath?' Lydia demanded, eyeing him suspiciously. 'I hardly know if I should like it, to be sure. I always associate it with sour-faced dowagers drinking nasty-tasting water and elderly gentlemen with gout immersing themselves in equally noxious-smelling pools.'

'You are not far wrong,' her husband admitted placidly.

It was clear that this answer did not please Mrs Savidge at all.

'Then why, in Heaven's name, should you want us to go there?' she asked, clearly astonished at him.

'I have just received a most interesting letter,' he explained, leaving her as confused as ever.

'A letter?' She cocked her head like a curious bird. 'From whom?'

'From a total stranger. He admits as much himself.'

Her interest was now truly caught. Lydia was a young woman who had not yet reached her twentieth birthday. She had grey eyes which might seem unremarkable at first glance but they sparkled with an innate intelligence and a keen curiosity. Her husband considered her almost pretty and thought himself lucky to have married her. He himself was a large man who appeared to be perpetually bored. But it would be unwise to take him for a fool, as many had found.

'Why would a stranger be writing to you?' Lydia asked him now. 'What can he want?'

'He requires our help.' John leaned back and looked over the document in his hand once more.

'*Our* help?' She snatched at the word immediately.

'Indeed.'

'Is it a murder?' The excitement in her voice was quite comical.

'No, my bloodthirsty madam,' he answered with a chuckle.

'What then?' She subsided, folding her arms across her breast and frowning.

'It is in the nature of a rescue.'

'A rescue?' she echoed. 'Kindly elucidate, my dear husband.'

'He wishes to procure our services in saving the reputation of his new bride.'

'That is decidedly odd.' She frowned. 'What kind of man marries a woman whose reputation appears to be conspicuously tainted?'

'It appears,' John said slowly, perusing the letter, 'that his wife is suspected of stealing a valuable necklace from a friend. Nothing was proven but she has been a virtual recluse for some years as a result of the general view that she is a thief.'

'How came he to meet and marry her, then?' Lydia asked reasonably.

'That,' he replied, 'he does not say.'

'Clearly he believes her to be innocent of the crime,' she stated. 'That must count for something.'

'Judging by his description,' John reflected, 'she is unquestionably a beauty, and it would seem that Mr — Rodrigo — quite dotes upon her.'

'Hardly an impartial judge, then,' she conceded. 'But I wonder what he expects us to do about this?'

'It is quite simple, really. Listen.'

He proceeded to read aloud from Gideon's epistle, which comprised quite three sheets of paper:

I understand from my acquaintance with Monsieur d'Almain that you and your wife possess a passion for justice and an uncanny ability to ferret out the truth of things. I beg you to consider my proposition to discover who stole the jewels in question and why they permitted Miss Halliwell to suffer such defamation for so many years.

'How many years ago did this famous robbery occur?' Lydia inquired.

'It has been seven years.'

'What!' Lydia gasped. 'We are to uncover a crime committed seven years ago?'

'You think it an impossible task?' He raised a brow, challenging her silently.

'I do not say that we cannot accomplish it,' she corrected him. 'But it does sound terribly difficult. And the young lady in question may well be guilty.'

'So what are we to tell the gentleman?'

Lydia hesitated, cogitating fiercely. At last she looked across at her husband and delivered her judgment.

'I think we should speak with Henri before we agree to anything.' Henri was her uncle, and a French Viscount — though he did not advertise this. Having lost everything in the Terror, he had immigrated to England and settled down to married bliss with a mere Miss Denton, who happened to be the half-sister of Lydia's mama. He earned his living as a designer of ornate jewellery for the wealthy and titled, and he and his wife now shared the large estate which had originally been purchased as a bridal gift for John and Lydia by the groom's ambitious father.

'An excellent idea, Madam Wife,' John said, nodding.

* * *

'Gideon Rodrigo is marrying a second time?'

This was Monsieur d'Almain's immediate response when John informed him of the letter that evening.

'To a Miss Anthea Halliwell,' John added.

'Not THE Anthea Halliwell!' Aunt Camilla exclaimed, apparently quite shocked.

'You know of her?' Lydia asked her aunt.

'My dear Lydia,' the older woman explained, 'it was a terrific scandal at the time. My old school friend, Mrs Hibbard, wrote to me about it. Miss Halliwell withdrew from all society, confining herself to her father's house. I had forgotten about it but hearing the name immediately restored my memory.'

'Miss Halliwell's father, Sir Harry, is a well-known gamester,' Henri put in. 'I fancy he has lost most of the fortune he inherited, and doubtless sold whatever jewels he could. That is probably how Gideon became acquainted with the daughter of the house.'

'Rodrigo,' Camilla murmured, turning the name over on her tongue with a decided tone of suspicion. 'It sounds rather . . . foreign.'

'Like d'Almain?' Lydia asked, amused at her aunt's English insularity — especially considering the fact that she was married to a Frenchman.

'Mr Rodrigo is a Jewish gentleman.'

'Most people would tell you,' John remarked, 'that the terms *Jew* and *gentleman* are quite incompatible.'

'They would be wrong,' Henri answered them at once. 'Gideon is a fine man and more of a gentleman than his bride's father — of that I am certain.'

'So, are we off to Bath, Mrs Savidge?' John asked his wife.

'I think we must,' she answered.

'It may not be murder,' he quizzed her, 'but it will help to offer a little diversion from the excessively dull life we lead here in Diddlington.'

'Please,' Aunt Camilla said with a shudder, 'do not be mentioning murder. We have had quite enough of that here!'

'Where will you stay in Bath?' Henri was curious.

'Mr Rodrigo informs me that he will hire a house for us near his own residence, and pay any expenses incurred in our . . . investigations.'

'That is very generous,' Lydia said admiringly.

'I still cannot believe that Rodrigo is marrying again.' Henri shook his head in disbelief. 'His daughter is turned seventeen, I believe. And it is my understanding that his first marriage was anything but happy.'

'He must be in love,' Lydia said doubtfully. 'I do hope that he and his Anthea will not be too tiresome. Lovers are ever a trial to deal with and usually quite vexatious.'

* * *

The next morning, John spent considerable time in drafting a reply to the Jew's unusual request. In accordance with his instructions, they would meet Mr Rodrigo at his house eight weeks from the date on which his letter had been written.

In the meantime, there was much to be done. Bath might have been eclipsed in splendour by the seaside resorts and other fashionable towns, but it was still a place where well-heeled persons of a certain class congregated. One would not wish to look like a dowd or a mushroom, and so a few new gowns for Lydia and a general refurbishment of his own wardrobe was essential before they could venture further afield. They had it on excellent authority that the Assembly Rooms were very grand and there were firework displays and other frivolities in Sydney Gardens. It was important to be prepared.

As for the task which Mr Rodrigo had set them, Lydia confided to her husband that her doubts grew as the time drew nearer. What, she wondered, had they got themselves into this time?

CHAPTER EIGHT: MARIAGE À LA MODE

The sun shone brightly down upon the many-tiered spire of St Bride's on the day that Anthea became Mrs Gideon Rodrigo. Navigating the busy streets of London, the stylish barouche belonging to the Guzmans seemed like a lost ship in a sea of restless humanity. Everywhere was noise and smell and confusion. It was a city alive and bustling, but curiously brash and unconcerned with the distress of a young lady who was facing an uncertain future. If Bath was like a carefully cultivated garden, London was a sprawling wilderness which undoubtedly concealed more than its share of danger.

'I love the city!' Mr Guzman exclaimed. 'Here, Miss Halliwell, is the beating heart of our nation.'

Judging by the smell, Anthea would have compared it to a rather less romantic part of the human anatomy. She did not voice her opinion aloud, however, merely smiling at the other two while trying not to think about what she was about to do.

To her surprise, they arrived on time and she stepped out onto the pavement, quaking inwardly even as she schooled herself to appear bland and unconcerned. The years of enforced restraint behind the walls of her father's residence stood her in good stead this day.

'Miss Halliwell.'

She would recognize that deep, smooth voice anywhere. Looking sideways, she perceived Gideon approaching. He was well turned out in a many-caped coat of dove grey over a matching riding coat. His boots were gleaming and his fashionable top hat had almost certainly come from Lock's. Was it her imagination, or was he even more handsome than she had remembered?

She greeted him diffidently, with a slight inclination of the head. Despite her best efforts, however, she must have betrayed some sign of nerves, for he immediately took her hands in a reassuring clasp.

'Courage, my dear,' he said softly. 'We are both of us sailing into uncharted waters, after all.'

She smiled to herself, realizing for the first time that he might well have his own doubts and apprehensions concerning what he was about to do. As she looked up at him, she saw a gleam in his eyes which made her catch her breath suddenly. It had been several years since any man had looked at her so, but not so long that she did not recognize it. Anthea knew that she was in good looks today, and admiration would not have been surprising. But this was something more: it was the look of strong desire.

He gave her his arm and led her into the church while the other two followed behind. But Anthea was now thoroughly overset. Was it possible? Had she merely imagined it? It was one thing to enter into a marriage of convenience with a relative stranger, and quite another to know that the man she was about to bind herself to with solemn vows and in the sight of God, might expect more from her than the performance of household duties.

Yet why should she be so surprised? Gideon was a man in the prime of life. It was not at all unreasonable to suppose that he would want a wife in every sense of the word. Only a simpleton would assume otherwise, and yet she had not seriously considered the matter before, being so caught up in what had seemed more pressing concerns. And now it was too late to withdraw.

The simple ceremony was over very quickly. Each of them repeated their vows in strong, clear voices, even though one of them at least felt anything but strong. Then they were standing outside in the sunshine once more. Everything was the same — except that she was no longer Miss Anthea Halliwell, but Mrs Gideon Rodrigo. The man beside her was no longer just a prosperous merchant, but her husband. For quite five minutes she heard her companions speaking without comprehending a word they said. She felt that she had become someone completely different. What would this new Anthea be like?

* * *

They repaired to Gideon's house in Mayfair for a light nuncheon. She had been curious to see the place ever since he had mentioned it on their memorable carriage ride together.

The house proved to be similar to his residence in Bath. It was neatly and simply furnished, but with everything of the first stare. His servants were clearly on their best behaviour as they greeted their new mistress. She was treated with great respect, tempered by looks of very natural curiosity. Anthea tried to come to terms with the fact that she would be expected to preside over more than one household.

They did not remain long in the house, for they were to spend the first fortnight of their married life with the Guzmans — who were much too insistent to be denied. After their meal — a light but refreshing confection of cream soup, oysters and cold meat — they returned to the barouche and were soon beyond the cramped streets of the town.

Seated beside her husband, Anthea tried to think of something to say, but soon found that there was no need to distress herself. Lavinia kept up a stream of conversation which was quite diverting and frequently unintentionally humorous.

'What a perfect day for a wedding,' she declared at one point.

'St Bride's is a lovely church,' Anthea said, feeling that she must contribute something.

'Oh yes!' Lavinia conceded. Turning to her husband, she added, 'The last time I was there was for your cousin's wedding. What was his name? Benjamin Braham, I think. Yes. It used to be *Abraham*, of course, but that is something which the family prefers to forget.'

'Now, Vinnie,' Mr Guzman chided her, 'you must not be so hard on them.'

'No indeed, Joseph.' She was eager to refute the suggestion. 'I meant no disrespect. After all, he is a war hero. Served with Wellington in Spain. Or was it Portugal? I forget. But so tragic.'

'How so?' Anthea could not refrain from asking.

'My dear' — Lavinia leaned forward in her eagerness to tell her story — 'it is the saddest thing. He came through the war without a scratch. Then after he returned to England he cut his foot on a shard of broken glass. Within a week it had turned gangrene and they were forced to decapitate his leg almost to the knee!'

Anthea struggled to keep from laughing at this absurd malapropism, but was almost undone by her husband, who could not refrain from commenting, 'Tragic indeed. But think how much worse it would have been had he cut his cheek. They might have amputated his head!'

Anthea could only disguise her laughter as a fit of coughing, which drew such tender solicitude from the older woman that she was quite ashamed of her mirth — involuntary though it had been.

CHAPTER NINE: UNEXPECTED FIRE

After dinner that evening, Anthea grew ever more apprehensive. Incredible though it seemed to her, this was her wedding night. What was she to expect? What did Gideon expect from her? She scarcely touched the gargantuan meal that had been prepared for them. Mercifully, no one seemed to notice.

Wandering into the drawing room behind the others, Anthea instinctively made her way to the pianoforte which stood prominently in one corner. By right, this was the music room, but as nobody played either the harp or piano so prominently on display, it had become merely a second and more intimate drawing room than the grander one at the front of the house.

She sat down at the instrument and began to play from memory: 'Voi che sapete' from *The Marriage of Figaro* by Mozart. This charming song by the love-struck page, Cherubino, seemed curiously appropriate tonight, and Anthea's voice — light, pleasing and perfectly suited to Mozart's music — vividly expressed the conflicting emotions of love so aptly described.

When she finished, there was a round of enthusiastic applause from her small audience. Gideon requested an encore, and she obliged with a short rondo by the same composer. They could not persuade her to attempt another song, and her hostess readily excused her by way of saying that she must be tired after so strenuous a day.

'Perhaps,' Gideon suggested, 'we might take a brief turn about the grounds before retiring. The moon is full tonight, so we should have no difficulty finding our way.'

Anthea hesitated briefly, then decided to accept his offer. It meant a temporary reprieve from the anxiety which gripped her at the thought of what might lie ahead on this, her first night as his wife. The other couple exchanged a significant glance which quite put her to the blush again, but they only urged the newlyweds not to be staying out too late.

In a very few moments, Anthea found herself passing out into the cool night air on the arm of her husband. They walked on in silence for several minutes, only the sound of their feet upon the gravel path disturbing the stillness. Did he feel as awkward as she was feeling? He certainly could not be as apprehensive. After all, he had the advantage in at least one respect — he had been married before.

The scene was set for romance: the moon riding high in a cloudless sky, the argent river flowing deep and unperturbed beneath them. It was a peaceful scene, quite at odds with the tumult within her. It was at once mysterious and enticing, made for secret trysts between lovers.

'Are you cold?' Gideon's voice, though low-toned, sounded like a trumpet blast in this solemn stillness.

'No.' She was striving to remain calm. 'It is quite comfortable tonight, I think.'

'Perhaps.'

More silence. She knew not what to say and hoped he did not hear her heart pounding. She felt she might swoon from sheer nervous agitation. She knew not what to expect, or what he expected from her.

'The Guzmans have been most kind and gracious to me,' she ventured at last. 'I like them very much.'

'I am glad of it.' He stopped, and she turned to look into his deep, dark eyes. 'They are fond of you as well. And they were undoubtedly correct in at least one observation today.'

'What is that?' she whispered, hardly able to speak for the sudden lump in her throat. Where had that come from?

'You are indeed the most beautiful bride that any groom could ask for.'

There was no mistaking the desire in his eyes now. While she stood, mesmerized into immobility, he lowered his head and brushed his lips gently against hers. She stiffened, a strange tingling sensation coursing through her from head to toe. He drew back at once, his hands falling away from her shoulders.

'Forgive me, my dear. Perhaps it is no surprise if you find my attentions . . . unpleasant.'

'Oh no!' She hastened to disabuse him of this misapprehension. Indeed she had been taken unaware by his kiss, but she had not been at all repelled. Quite the contrary.

'You expected,' he asked gently, 'that our marriage would be one in name only?'

'I had not considered the matter before today,' she answered truthfully.

'I would not force anything distasteful upon you, Anthea.' He was serious, perhaps chagrined.

'Your kiss was not . . . distasteful to me.'

'No?'

'No.'

They were very near the bench where Anthea had sat only days before to view the same panorama by daylight. He led her the few steps to it and they sat side by side.

'If you wish to convince me of that,' he quizzed, 'you must make a greater effort, Mrs Rodrigo.'

'What — what do you mean, sir?'

'You may call me Gideon, you know.' He smiled. 'You have done so before and, after all, we are married now.'

'What do you mean, Gideon?' she rephrased the question.

To her consternation, he raised his right hand to her face and softly traced the line of her cheek with one outstretched finger. When that finger reached the point of her chin, he slowly tilted her head to look at him again. Anthea was more confused than ever. His touch was having the most unexpected effect upon her, making her breath catch in her throat and creating a feeling of light-headedness which was oddly exhilarating.

'If you would make a believer of me, then kiss me, Anthea.'

'Kiss you?'

'Kiss me.'

He clearly expected her to obey this amazing request. Slowly Anthea closed the gap between his lips and her own. Hesitating for a moment, she pressed her mouth to his but drew back almost immediately.

'Surely you can do better than that,' he mocked.

'Can I?'

'I am sure of it.'

'Shall I kiss you again, then?'

'If you would be so kind.'

The entire situation was so fantastic — the moonlit night, the man beside her, his outrageous suggestions — that everything seemed strangely unreal. Perhaps her new husband was a lunatic! If so, she had better humour him. As if in a dream, she drew closer and kissed him once more. But this time he did not allow her to withdraw so quickly. Instead, he parted her lips with his tongue and gave her a very thorough lesson in what a kiss should be. She was not certain how long it lasted, was not even aware of when she began to return it, but when it ended she was held in a very firm embrace with her arms around his neck.

'That was much better,' he whispered.

'Shall I kiss you once more?' she asked hopefully.

'Do you wish to?'

'Yes,' she admitted. 'I do.'

They spent a considerable amount of time on that bench, and Anthea was soon quite confused as to who was kissing whom — and who was enjoying the experience the most. Gideon traced a line of kisses along the length of her throat, making her moan softly as a kind of fire seemed to be slowly but surely melting her body, along with her resistance. He paused briefly before his lips moved downward to more enticing regions. Then, quite abruptly, he raised his head and stood up.

'What is the matter?' she demanded, feeling suddenly bereft.

'I think we should return to the house.'

He reached down and pulled her up beside him — but only to draw her into his arms once more. It took them some considerable time to reach the house, their progress impeded by several kisses and — at least on Anthea's part — a mounting excitement which totally eclipsed her earlier apprehension.

The Guzmans had long since retired, so they made their way through the house unmolested until they came to the door of Gideon's bedchamber. He opened it, and Anthea went in without any hesitation.

When his arms closed around her this time, Anthea needed no request for her kisses. She could hardly bear to tear her lips away from his. When his hands began slow and deliberate caresses, and she could no longer be unaware of his fully aroused passions, she finally managed to whisper, 'I think — I am almost sure . . . Are you seducing me, Mr Rodrigo?'

'That is my intention, Mrs Rodrigo,' he murmured, his lips teasing hers.

'Oh.'

'Have you any objection, my sweet?'

'Not at all,' she confessed.

He drew a deep, shuddering breath. 'If I do anything tonight which you dislike, sweetheart,' he said against her neck, 'you have only to say the word and I will stop at once.'

But she was impatient with talk. Having pushed aside his shirt, she was preoccupied with the tantalizing taste of his bare flesh and did not dignify this absurd comment with an answer. Any worries she had ever harboured were long past, and she submitted eagerly to his increasing demands. Indeed, she wondered what could ever have alarmed her in the thought of consummating her marriage. Nothing had ever filled her with such delightful . . . incredible . . . aahhh! . . . pleasure.

* * *

It was much, much later that Anthea lay, sated and serene, with her head upon her husband's chest and his body wrapped around hers in a manner which was surprisingly comfortable. Some part of her mind registered a kind of bemused wonder at what had passed between them tonight. The things he had *done*! The things *she* had done! The things they had done *together*! She was certain that she should be shocked. She should blush for her wanton indulgence in passions which had been perfectly unknown to her before. Her complete surrender and absolute enjoyment must surely betoken a want of sensibility — a moral turpitude contrary to all she had been taught to reverence. Yet she had done nothing wrong, committed no sin. Even so stern a moralist as St. Paul had proclaimed the marriage bed 'undefiled' and what man and wife did behind its veil not open to public censure. And what if her pleasure in her husband was excessive? That must be better than to find no pleasure in him at all.

'You did not ask me to stop.'

Gideon's voice interrupted her thoughts, and she raised her head to look into his smiling face as she recalled his words earlier.

'I did not want you to stop,' she said truthfully.

'Not even once?'

'Not even once,' she assured him. 'Not for an instant.'

He looked remarkably relaxed and more handsome than any man had a right to be.

'You are satisfied with your seduction, then?'

'Completely satisfied.' To emphasize her point, she kissed him again, then continued with a little less confidence, 'And are *you* satisfied, now that you have seduced your wife so thoroughly?'

'There is not a man in England — in all the world — who can boast of greater pleasure than I have found in my beautiful bride.'

'I never dreamed it could be like this.'

'Like what?' he asked, nibbling her ear.

'I never expected,' she explained, 'that I should find such happiness with you.'

'How odd.' His arm tightened about her. 'I have never doubted for a moment that you would make me supremely happy.'

'You are quizzing me again,' she accused, pressing still closer. His body was a magnet, drawing her inexorably to him, and she was glad to discard any lingering trace of shyness or restraint, no longer even amazed at her own temerity.

'Am I?' He planted another passionate kiss on very willing lips.

'But what shall I do now?' she asked.

'Whatever pleases you,' he replied suggestively, 'will doubtless please me as well.'

'No, no.' She tried to suppress a giggle. 'I do not know the proper etiquette for a married lady, when it comes to sharing her husband's bed. Shall I return to my own chamber, or remain here with you?'

He appeared to give the matter serious consideration.

'That,' he explained with mock solemnity, 'is a private matter which must be decided between husband and wife. I shall leave the matter entirely up to you, my dear.'

'What do you wish me to do?' she insisted.

'Oh no,' he protested. 'You shall not catch me out with such stratagems, sweetheart. I shall only ask you what *you* wish to do.'

'I wish to stay with my husband,' she said promptly.

'Before you commit yourself to such a rash course of action,' he said, tightening his hold, 'I must warn you that you are not like to get much sleep if you remain in my bed tonight.'

'I shall be happy for you to keep me up all night,' she said saucily, her pulse racing even faster at the thought.

'And,' he added against her lips, 'if you spend the night with me, I may well expect you to do so every night in future.'

'Every night?' Her words came out with a slight gasp.

'Every night,' he said firmly. 'So what is your decision, my love? Do you stay or go?'

'Gideon,' she said, 'I have no intention of leaving your bed. I am staying.'

'Every night?' he repeated.

'Every night,' she vowed.

It was a promise she would very much enjoy keeping.

CHAPTER TEN: FAMILY MATTERS

The fortnight at Richmond Hill was a time of discovery and wonder. Anthea could not recall a period of her life when she had been so happy. It was so very different from anything she had known before, this sense of being attuned to Gideon in almost everything. There were times when their gaze would meet and the fire of passion in his eyes would ignite an answering spark within her which threatened a conflagration that could only be extinguished in his arms.

Her own lack of restraint continued to amaze her, but her bridegroom did not seem at all displeased. With each day that passed, it was as if she cut more of the strings that bound her to her old life, her old self. Gone was the despair and the crushed spirit she had endured. With Gideon, she began to feel as if anything might be possible. It was a kind of magic, and she was afraid to question it, lest the spell be broken.

As for Gideon, he luxuriated in the unexpected gift of their shared passion — a state of euphoria he had thought only opium eaters enjoyed. On their wedding night, her complete capitulation was as unexpected as it was satisfying. They had both been swept away on a torrent of raw emotion which seemed as if it would never abate. His first marriage had been a kind of purgatory in which neither partner found pleasure or happiness. He had endured his own private prison but was now free at last and learning that it was one thing to have a wife who merely tolerated his attentions, and one who was an equal partner in pleasure and who delighted him as no other woman had ever done.

They spent many hours talking and getting to know one another better, so that their union became not merely a physical one, but one where both experienced a bond of heart and mind as well. Of course it could not last for ever. Bath awaited them, and they must go home at last.

* * *

Their return was much less dramatic than their departure from the city. The carriage drew up outside the house in Charles Street, and her husband assisted her to alight. Rachel was eager to greet them, pronouncing that they looked prodigiously happy. Marriage, she considered, suited them.

'My dear,' Gideon said, embracing her and playfully pinching one cheek, 'you do not look as if you have been pining for your father.'

'We have been vastly entertained by all the scandalous rumours regarding your sudden disappearance with a mysterious young woman!' Her laughter was youthful and gay as she led the way inside.

'I never heard of such things,' Mrs Norton said primly. 'Shameful, I call it. And you should be mindful of your tongue, miss!'

'Oh pooh!' Rachel dismissed her objection.

'You are quite right, Mrs Norton.' Anthea's support was an olive branch which the housekeeper was shrewd enough to recognize and accept with good grace.

'If anyone says a word about it in my hearing,' the older woman said, raising her chin, 'they'll get the sharp edge of my tongue, I can tell you! A fine thing for folks to be bandying tales of their betters about the town.'

'I shall try to be a good wife and a helpful stepmother to you, Rachel.'

'I had rather you be my friend.'

'I think you could find no better friend in all the world than Anthea,' Gideon said.

'You are quite impartial, I see,' his daughter teased.

'Yes.' Anthea put in. 'After examining the matter very carefully, he is convinced that I am the perfect wife.'

Rachel read them the short entry in the *Chronicle* which speculated that Mr R and Miss H were headed for Gretna Green. Gideon chuckled and commented that they must think him a fine buffle-head to flee all the way to Scotland. A notice of their marriage in the paper soon put an end to such surmises. The Rodrigo family began to settle into their new roles without much beyond stares and whispers from those they passed, who likely saw them as if they were characters who had stepped out of the pages of the *Minerva Press*.

The two Rodrigo ladies busied themselves in the acquisition of new wardrobes: one for the woefully ill-equipped Anthea and another wardrobe suitable for a young lady entering upon her first season in society. Anthea's days back in town were now spent in a never-ending round of visits to the finest shops in Milsom and Bond streets. Morning gowns, afternoon gowns, evening gowns, bonnets, capes, undergarments. It was a paradise on earth for those seeking to be fashionable, and soon Rachel and her stepmother were (to quote Mrs Norton), 'as thick as thieves, the pair of them.'

* * *

While the ladies indulged themselves in numerous personal acquisitions, Gideon was occupied in other less pleasant pursuits. He was resolved that something must be done about Anthea's father. Sir Harry simply could not be allowed to sink into a gin-soaked stupor in Avon Street with the likes of Mrs Pomfrit.

On a fine April day he had made his way to the lady's lodgings, where Sir Harry was soon to be ensconced. After knocking on the door, it had not taken long for the mistress of the household to answer. She was a heavily rouged woman of indeterminate age and questionable class. At first she mistook Gideon for a tradesman who was dunning her gentleman friend for unpaid bills and tried to shut the door in his face. He quickly disabused her, however.

Having made his identity known to her, he got little encouragement initially.

'Son-in-law!' she exclaimed. 'The filthy Jew? Lawks!'

The interior of the house was not inviting, with worn furnishings and a stale, unwholesome smell which might emanate from the much-stained carpet or from the lady herself. She must have been handsome once, but her charms were as faded as her abode.

'What do yer want, Shylock?' she asked him.

'I am hoping that you might consider severing your — connection — with my wife's father.'

'Think I'm not good enough for him, eh?' she demanded. 'And who are you — a crucifying knave of a Jew — to be judging a decent Christian woman like me?'

He sighed. Once he would have risen up in righteous anger at this, but years of harsh words and condescending looks from those who considered themselves superior to one of his tribe had hardened him to such insults. Having heard it all before, he was practically impervious now. He remained courteous but determined. After all, he was not ashamed of who and what he was — and had less to repent of than the wretched female before him.

'Naturally,' he said with a smile, 'I would not expect you to make such a noble sacrifice without some form of compensation.'

'Compensation?' The word caught her attention and her manner changed abruptly. Belligerence was quickly replaced by avarice.

'I realize that you would be losing your lover and your —
protector — as well,' he answered, choosing his words with care.

'Ah sir!' She looked mournfully at him, feigning a sensibility she surely did not possess. 'So sad as it would be to be
parted from one so dear . . .'

More of this delicate manoeuvring had to be got through
before they came to the crux of the matter: the price. He ventured a sum which he expected would be too small for her to
accept, fishing for a more exact knowledge of her monetary
expectations. She gently chided him, saying that he surely
could not suppose that anything so paltry could ease the
pains of love denied. More angling produced a figure which
was at once more than he liked and less than he had feared he
would be parting with. In the end, he left her with a promise
on his part to have a sum of three thousand pounds delivered
to her the following day, and, on her side, a tacit agreement
to send Sir Harry packing this very evening.

Now he was on his way to see his father-in-law, having
been reliably informed that Mrs Pomfrit had indeed given him
his *conge* the previous evening. In New King Street he purposed
to complete the second portion of his campaign. Sir Harry
should by now be in quite a quandary. He was on the point
of being evicted from his current residence and his fortunes
were definitely at their lowest ebb. Now was the perfect time
to confront him, when his choices were too few for him to
object very strenuously to any reasonable proposal for his relief.

The last time he had seen his wife's father was six months
previously, when he had been solicited by the tenant who
then had been eager to ingratiate himself with the wealthy
merchant whose assistance he sought. He would not be so
welcoming today.

* * *

At his knock, the door was opened by a frightened-looking
maid whose eyes almost started from their sockets as she recognized him.

At his request to see her master, she folded herself into an awkward curtsey and whisked herself away toward the rear of the house. She returned, red-faced and flustered, to deliver a message:

'If you please, sir, the master says to tell you to get the 'ell out of 'is house. He has nothing to say to you.'

He was too irritated to be amused, and brushed past her, making his way down the corridor toward the small sitting room he remembered from his previous visits. The house had the air of a place about to be abandoned, with little furniture and nothing adorning the walls. The little maid danced along behind him, begging him not to cause any trouble.

Gideon found Sir Harry sprawled upon a low sofa, one leg outstretched along its length and the other resting upon the floor. At sight of his visitor, however, he drew himself up with surprising speed.

'How dare you come here, sir?' He sat rigidly before him. 'Damned impudence!'

'I thought it best to speak with you before you are expelled from this residence,' Gideon answered calmly. 'I collect your next residence is like to be the gutter.'

'That is no concern of yours.' He slowly rose to stand before him.

'It is of concern to my wife, however.'

This gentle rejoinder was not well received.

'Your wife!' The older man looked positively apoplectic. 'I do not know her, sir.'

'Do you know your daughter, then?'

'My daughter is dead to me.'

'Is she so?'

'That you, of all men, should betray me in such a manner!' Sir Harry struck a pose. 'To have abducted and . . . defiled my only child. You, in whom I placed such trust and whom I regarded almost as a friend.'

'Whether you approve or not, I am Anthea's lawful husband.' Gideon was growing tired of his father-in-law's histrionics. 'But let us not bandy words, sir. I have assisted you in financial matters on more than one occasion, and I am here to offer my help once more.'

'I am sure I do not know what you mean.' He looked down his patrician nose in feigned surprise.

'You are dished up,' Gideon said with crude accuracy. 'Your creditors are dunning you and you have not the means to pay the rent on this house. Your lightskirt has abandoned you and you are alone without any immediate recourse. Now do you understand my meaning?'

Sir Harry dropped back on the sofa, sulking and pouting like a petulant schoolboy.

'And what is that to you?'

'Whatever you may think of me, do me the justice of believing that I love your daughter.'

'Do you?' He gave a grunt. 'I suppose you always meant to have her.'

'I wanted her from the first moment I saw her,' he answered honestly. 'And I would have been a fool not to have grasped at the opportunity to wed her when it presented itself.'

'By God, sir,' the older man cried, reddening, 'if I were a few years younger, I would take great pleasure in knocking you down and teaching you a deal more respect.'

'I doubt you would be successful,' Gideon said, cutting through the man's bluster. 'I have sparred with Mendoza in the past and acquitted myself very well.'

Perhaps Sir Harry recalled that the Jews were among the finest pugilists in the country, and that his son-in-law's words were unlikely to be an idle boast, or it might have been that he could not deny his case was desperate.

'What do you expect me to do?' he asked.

'I ask only that you make an attempt to be more circumspect in future. I will arrange for the rent on this house to be paid and a small amount set aside for your household expenses.' Gideon seated himself in a chair facing the other man, much as he had done in their past negotiations. 'Consider it in the nature of a dowry. For the sake of my wife, I would prefer that her father be at least respectable. But if you decide otherwise, you may go to the Devil. It is for you to accept or reject my offer.'

'Am I to be kept by a Jew?'

Gideon shrugged. 'Such arrangements are not uncommon among members of the *ton*, I believe.'

'And what next will you ask of me, sirrah? Tell me that!'

'Sir,' Gideon replied, looking him in the eye, 'the only thing I have ever wanted from you, I already have.'

In the end, there was little that Harry Halliwell could do. With ill grace and far less gratitude than his benefactor deserved, he acquiesced. He declared that he would never set foot in his daughter's house — a burden which Gideon found most easy to bear — and grumbled about selling his soul to Mammon, but there was little doubt that he was relieved to yield to this last necessity, however grim.

CHAPTER ELEVEN: THE GAMES BEGIN

The first view of Bath definitely did not disappoint, Lydia decided. Awash in the golden light of a fresh May afternoon, following close on a slight shower of rain, the city had a glow that emphasized the classical elegance of the buildings, with the Abbey church rising up to point the way forward.

'It is quite lovely,' she declared, with a sigh of relief.

'What did you expect?' John inquired, chuckling. 'A collection of half-ruined hovels?'

'Not at all,' she protested. 'And perhaps some might find its restrained elegance less than interesting. But it seems curiously reassuring. As if no tread of violence might disrupt its solid placidity.'

'Staid, stolid and unbelievably dull,' he summed up for her.

'So say you.' She sniffed.

'But we know that not everything here is as tranquil as it might seem on first acquaintance.'

'We are aware of at least one theft, you would say.'

'And who can tell what else may lurk behind these neat stone facades?'

'I did not know that you went in for melodrama,' she chided, her lips twitching slightly. 'Have you been reading Byron again?'

'Vixen!' he replied, giving her an affectionate hug.

'We shall see what dastardly secrets we can uncover. Who is hiding behind the nearest arras in order to spring out on poor Hamlet, one wonders?'

The house to which Mr Rodrigo had directed them in his reply to John's letter was located only five doors away from his own residence, so it would be easy for them to meet and discuss how their work might be progressing. It was a fine residence, if furnished in a rather Spartan style. Quite suitable for a few weeks' residence in the town.

They were to meet their mysterious patron on the following morning. Lydia was very much looking forward to this particular introduction, and she was eaten up with curiosity to see the new Mrs Rodrigo. That would go a long way to deciding how they might proceed.

* * *

The morning brought a heavy downpour, but to their relief it had dissipated by the time they were ready to make their way along the street to their much-anticipated destination.

A loud knock brought the housekeeper bustling to the door. She looked taken aback by the two strangers before her, but Lydia quickly informed her that they were here at the express invitation of her master.

Mrs Norton stepped back to facilitate their entry into the house and was about to leave them while she informed Mr Rodrigo of their arrival, but she was forestalled by the arrival of a young damsel who had been watching from the stairs.

'I'll take them to Papa,' she announced, skipping forward and looking them up and down in a very interested manner which might have disconcerted or offended some, but which Lydia and John found quite amusing.

'It is very kind of you, Miss . . .' Lydia's voice trailed off, awaiting elucidation.

'I'm Rachel,' the girl supplied. 'Papa has been waiting for you, and I've been dying to meet you myself!'

'Have you?' John permitted himself a slight smile at this.

'Oh yes!' she carolled, leading them down the hall as she spoke. 'I believe Anthea was rather upset when he told her of his plans, but I think it sounds like great fun. Almost as good as having a couple of Bow Street Runners on the case!'

By now they had arrived at the door of a good-sized and well-appointed apartment which appeared to be a drawing room. There were two occupants: a handsome man with an air of authority about him, and a stunningly beautiful young woman who eyed them somewhat nervously.

'Great God!' Lydia exclaimed involuntarily. 'You truly *are* a Beauty.'

At this, the gentleman's lips curved upward in an attractive smile, while the golden goddess before them looked as if she were confronting a curious animal whose precise nature she could not quite make out. She clung to her husband's arm as if it were a lifeline and she a drowning mariner.

'Forgive my wife,' John stated with cool unconcern. 'There are times when her mouth produces speech which her head may not fully approve.'

'I beg your pardon,' Lydia stammered, wishing she had not lost control of her tongue on so momentous an occasion. They must think her the greatest simpleton.

'May I assume,' Gideon Rodrigo answered, coming forward, 'that you are Mr and Mrs John Savidge?'

'At your service, sir.' John smiled and bowed in acknowledgement.

'You are very young,' the older man commented with a little pardonable misgiving.

'"*Let no man despise thy youth*," as St Paul said to Timothy,' Mr Savidge quoted blithely.

'It is what everyone says when first we meet them,' Lydia added. 'But I assure you that, in spite of appearances to the contrary, we are well able to accomplish the tasks we are set.'

Gideon looked at them more closely and seemed to come to a decision.

'I am informed that you have brought more than one murderer to justice.' He paused significantly before continuing, 'I believe that you are just the persons I need to find the truth and clear away the cloud that overshadows my wife's life.'

'Really, Gideon,' Mrs Rodrigo protested, 'there is no need to go to such trouble. I have lived with this for almost seven years, and now that I am your wife, I am too happy to be over-burdened by what other people may think.'

'But,' Lydia interjected, 'if you have been unjustly accused, Mrs Rodrigo, then someone who has committed a serious crime has gone unpunished while you have taken the blame for their misdeeds.'

'That cannot be allowed to continue,' John added with grim finality.

'This is all quite new to me,' young Rachel put in at this point. 'What is it that Thea is supposed to have done? I have heard of her seclusion, but no one has ever explained its origin. I know that Papa has been keeping something from me, but surely I have as much right to know as anyone!'

'It is something I would prefer to forget,' Anthea admitted.

'But the citizens of Bath will not forget,' Gideon reminded her. 'You will never be able to take your proper place in society until this is settled once and for all.'

'I know that it cannot be easy for you, Mrs Rodrigo,' Lydia said quietly, 'but I think you need to tell us your story if we are to have some idea of where to begin in our endeavours.'

'It all seems so hopeless.' Anthea put up her hand as if to ward off further argument. 'What can you hope to gain by digging up something that was buried seven years ago?'

'What if,' John suggested, 'it was buried alive?'

'I beg your pardon?' the lady asked.

'Just because we do not see something,' he said, pressing home his point, 'that does not mean that it is gone. Hidden sins are no less real or deadly because they are not exposed.

As long as this remains unresolved, there can be no peace or lasting contentment for you, ma'am — nor for your children, should you and your husband be blessed with them.'

This argument clearly impressed the lady, for she ceased her protest and said, 'Very well, then. I will tell you what I can recall of that time. Most of it is as clear to me now as the day on which it all began.'

'So I would imagine.'

'Take your time, dearest,' her husband said, placing an arm about her shoulders as they sat side by side on the sofa.

Anthea drew a deep breath and closed her eyes momentarily while she gathered her thoughts together.

'It all began,' she said, 'with a ball.'

* * *

Anthea was a young lady of nineteen, enjoying a most delightful season. Indeed, she was the brightest star of Bath society that year. Although Papa's gaming debts had forced them to move again the year before, he had a sudden run of luck which enabled her to purchase the finest gowns and to outshine all the other ladies at the balls and assemblies.

Crispin Flitwick, a dashing young captain recently returned from the battlefields of Spain, was paying her marked attentions and it was not long before she received and accepted the expected offer of his hand and heart. Many young ladies envied her for snaring so fine a catch, and she had been pardonably proud of her triumph.

'There was to be a special ball in honour of the recent peace,' she recalled, 'and Georgina and I were in raptures over our new dresses and the jewels we planned to wear.'

'Georgina?' Lydia asked.

'Miss Georgina Shields,' Anthea explained. 'She was the only child of a wealthy father who had no title but vast estates in Derbyshire.'

Georgina was a beauty in her own right, but where Anthea was tall and blonde, her friend was rather petite, short and vivacious, with dark brown ringlets and matching eyes. An accomplished flirt, she was a favourite with many of the gentlemen. Anthea was rather more reserved, but her gentle demeanour and sly sense of humour endeared her even to those who were not as gifted.

Miss Shields had a particularly fine collection of jewels, worth — as anyone would tell you — a king's ransom. One of these was a necklace of rich red rubies and sparkling diamonds: a gift from her father, which Anthea considered rather too gaudy for her own taste.

One evening, as they were preparing to attend a party at a friend's house, Georgina complained that the clasp on this necklace was faulty, though it had only recently been mended. She removed it and handed it to Anthea, who saw nothing wrong. Georgina insisted, however, that her dear friend keep it safe for her for a few days until it could be repaired, as she did not wish to risk losing it. Instead, Anthea gladly loaned her one of her own necklaces — a much less grand affair of garnets which had been a favourite of her late mama.

'The floor in my bedchamber had a loose board beneath the carpet which acted as a secret trinket box, and which no one but I and my father knew of,' she added, for the benefit of her listeners. 'I showed it to Georgina, who seemed quite intrigued by it and said that she must have a carpenter fashion something similar for her.'

For two more days, the necklace remained in Anthea's bedchamber. On the night of the ball, however, Georgina insisted that she simply must wear it, despite its flaw. Nothing else would do. Of course, when the board was raised, the necklace had gone.

'How terrible!' Rachel interjected at this point.

'Aside from yourself and Miss Shields,' Lydia asked practically, 'who else knew where the necklace was hidden?'

'Apart from Papa, nobody,' Anthea said. 'Georgina swore that she had told no one, and I am very sure that I did not.'

'One of the servants might have discovered it in cleaning,' John suggested.

'Most unlikely.' Anthea shook her head sadly. 'It was too well hidden. After all, I had kept several of my own valuables there for almost a year and nothing had ever gone missing before. But there was worse yet to come.'

'What could be worse than that?' Rachel was agog with curiosity.

It was only a few days later, Anthea told them, when Georgina's father received a note from Mr Herschel, a local jeweller who had recently repaired the necklace. Herschel requested that Mr Shields and his daughter attend him at his shop, as he had something for them which might be of interest. When they arrived, he handed them the necklace without any preamble, and then explained that a woman had come to see him at a very late hour one evening and attempted to sell him the jewels for a ridiculously dear sum. Of course, having recognized the necklace as the one he had recently handled — and being, besides, an honest man — he refused this offer.

The lady, who was heavily veiled, asked him to keep the necklace for a day or two before he decided against it irrevocably. He agreed, but immediately determined to inform the rightful owners.

'But if he did not see the lady,' Gideon inquired logically, 'how could anyone be certain that it was you?'

'He could see that she was tall and blonde,' Anthea pointed out. 'He could not swear that it was I, but he could not say definitely that it was not.'

Added to this was the fact that when Herschel asked her name, she began to say 'Miss Hal—' Stopping abruptly, she then answered that she was Miss Haliburton. He did not doubt that she was about to say that her name was Halliwell.

'The evidence against you was very strong,' Lydia commented, frowning.

'And yet,' Rachel announced with confidence, 'I know that Anthea did not do it.'

'How can you be sure of that?' Anthea smiled in spite of herself.

'Well, you may have some fusty notions,' Rachel declared, leaning forward to touch her stepmother's hand briefly, 'and you can be tiresome and conventional. But you would never betray a friend in such a fashion.'

'Thank you, my dear.' Anthea almost choked on the words. It seemed incredible that both her husband and his daughter were convinced of her innocence.

'What I cannot understand,' John Savidge put in, 'is how you managed to escape the hangman.'

'Georgina would not bring charges against me,' Anthea responded. 'Indeed, she was very gracious and said that she was sure that we were in financial distress. Since the necklace had been recovered, she was prepared to forget the matter.'

'And did she?' Lydia asked somewhat drily. It sounded an unlikely thing for any young woman to do.

'No.' Anthea compressed her lips. 'It was the end of our friendship.'

'Miss Shields forgave you because of your financial situation,' Lydia said slowly, considering the matter. 'But you have told us that your father was doing quite well at the time.'

'Yes,' she agreed. 'He was pretty flush in the pocket in those days.'

'So what gave your friend the impression that things were otherwise?'

'I do not know.' Anthea's brows drew together as she pondered this. 'Local gossip, perhaps?'

'Perhaps,' Lydia echoed, but did not look convinced.

'And does Miss Shields still live here in Bath?' It was John's turn to ask a question now.

'She . . .' Anthea cleared her throat before continuing, 'She married Crispin a few months afterward, and they now live in Derbyshire.'

'Married Crispin!' Rachel squealed, goggling at her.

Anthea nodded.

'She married the gentleman who had been engaged to you . . .'

'He was most courteous while explaining why he wished to be released from his . . . obligation to me.' Anthea actually chuckled now, looking back and recalling his awkward and comically hypocritical valedictory address. It was worthy of the Reverend Mr Collins himself. 'And, for myself, I had no desire to wed a man whose faith in me was so easily relinquished.'

'What a poltroon!' Rachel was angrier than Anthea. 'You are well rid of him, Thea.'

'I quite agree.'

'Had you any suspicion who had taken the jewels?' John wanted to know.

'For some time I thought that it might have been Papa.' Anthea reddened uncomfortably. 'But he was so certain that *I* was guilty that he could not bring himself to speak to me for some months afterward. Then I thought . . .' her voice trailed off.

'You thought?' Lydia insisted.

'It seemed to me that there could have been only one other person who could have taken it.' She stopped.

'Who might that have been?'

'Georgina.'

CHAPTER TWELVE: AN IMPOSSIBLE SITUATION

'Mrs Rodrigo is right, of course,' John said to Lydia later that evening, as they lay side by side in their bedchamber at their lodgings.

'There certainly seems to be no mystery here as to the identity of the thief,' his wife agreed. 'The difficulty will be in proving it after all these years, and with precious little to attest to her guilt.'

'Not to mention the fact that there appears to be little, if any, motive for her crime!'

'I would not say that.' Lydia caught her lips between her teeth and squinted slightly in concentration.

John turned his head slightly, raising an eyebrow in gentle interrogation. 'What motive can you discern?'

'One of the oldest in the history of human motives. Jealousy.' She sighed softly, adding, 'It is not good to covet your neighbour's possessions. Often it is not even that one needs or wants what another has. It is merely that human beings have a tendency to compare what they have to that of others, and if the others have even one item more, they are as aggrieved as if they were deprived of food and drink.'

John lay back and stared at the ceiling while pondering this. 'Hmmm,' he murmured, 'I see what you mean. Miss

Shields was in pursuit of the captain, who was betrothed to Mrs Rodrigo — then Miss Halliwell.'

'If she could discredit Anthea — ruin her reputation — then it was all too likely that the young officer would lose no time in asking her to release him from his promise.'

'And Miss Shields,' John continued, 'would be there to console the disillusioned gentleman . . .'

'And walk off with the prize she so much coveted: a dashing young husband.'

'While Anthea was left to shame and social ostracism.'

'A neat plan,' Lydia summed up the situation. 'If she actually did contrive it.'

They were both silent for a few moments.

'I wish I might meet her,' John said slowly. 'Then I would have some notion of her character and of what she is capable.'

'I wonder,' Lydia said, turning on her side the better to converse, 'whether she ever visits Bath these days. Even if she does not live here, it might be a place where she would come, if only to see old acquaintances.'

'Well,' her husband answered, 'that should be a matter which is easily settled.'

'How so?'

'We have only to pay a visit to the Lower and Upper Assembly Rooms, have a chat with the Master of Ceremonies, and perhaps leaf through the Book of Intelligence which lists arriving visitors.'

'Is there such a book?' Lydia was forced to confess her ignorance of this salient point.

'Yes indeed,' John hastened to assure her. 'In fact, we must add our own names if we are to be considered at all tonnish.'

'Tomorrow?'

He nodded. 'It will not do to delay this important social tradition.'

* * *

The morning found them sauntering toward the Assembly Rooms to see what they might discover. Lydia felt a curious sensation of anticipation and assurance. She was convinced that they were about to take their first tentative step to solving this puzzle.

The Lower Rooms were decidedly unspectacular, but Lydia was suitably impressed by the Upper Rooms built by Wood the Younger. The ballroom was one hundred feet in length, she was informed, and lit at night by five immense chandeliers, giving it a most grandiose air. They chatted with the Master of Ceremonies, and she only wished that she had been able to meet the legendary Beau Nash in his heyday.

Pausing to enter their names in the book, they took a few minutes to read the names of some of the other visitors who had come to the city most recently. Aristocrats, country mushrooms, parsons and every person with pretensions to gentility were all represented in these pages. It was not long before John nudged Lydia, pointing to an entry made only a few days previously:

Captain and Mrs Crispin Flitwick

'You see, my dear Lydia,' John said with mock solemnity, 'it sometimes pays to observe even the most staid traditions.'

'So it does,' she agreed with an impish grin. 'But where, dear husband, do we go from here?'

'An obligatory visit to the Pump Room is in order, I believe.'

'Ah yes!' Lydia grimaced slightly. 'I have been warned about the famous Bath Waters.'

'Well,' he murmured, 'we must gird our loins and acquit ourselves like men of valour.'

'Easy for you, perhaps,' she replied.

'We may encounter our quarry there.'

'But remember,' she protested gently, 'we have never seen them and will not recognize them from Adam.'

They strolled arm-in-arm out into the bright sunlight, and he directed their course toward the famed Pump Room.

Arriving there some minutes later, they both decided to get one more tradition out of the way. The warnings which Lydia had been given concerning the noxious waters of Bath had not been exaggerated. Were it not for good manners, she would have spit it out at once, but as that would have been most improper and inelegant, she managed one swallow before determining that it would be her last. John did better, downing a whole cup and finishing off Lydia's.

'This is more likely to kill than to cure the infirm,' she declared, wishing she might drink something else to expunge the taste from her mouth and memory.

'You are not the first to say so,' a cool but attractive voice spoke from nearby.

John and Lydia turned their heads the better to behold the speaker. She was a woman of a certain age — perhaps sixty or so — who was dressed in a subdued variation on the latest London fashions. Her name, they discovered, was Mrs Lynford.

Getting past the obligatory introductions, they soon learned that she lived just a stone's throw away from their lodgings. When they explained that they were visiting the Rodrigos, she cocked an interested head.

'The Rodrigos . . .' She smiled, commenting with some amusement, 'They have certainly provided the city with a good deal of entertainment lately. Their elopement was a nine-day wonder, I assure you.'

'Has there been a great deal of gossip?' Lydia asked her.

'My dear young lady, were it not for gossiping, many of my friends and neighbours would be quite at a loss for something to do.'

'Mrs Rodrigo,' John said pointedly, 'seems to be prone to scandalous behaviour.'

Their new friend did not pretend to misunderstand him.

'If you refer to that business of her friend's necklace,' she said, shaking her head, 'I have always been of the opinion that Anthea was innocent.'

'Did her friends all desert her at that time?'

'Many of them did, Mrs Savidge,' she admitted somewhat grimly. 'Of course, it is not altogether strange that they should. I did attempt to call on her myself on two occasions but was told that Miss Halliwell was not receiving visitors.'

'We understand that the friend whose necklace was purloined is actually in Bath at the moment,' Lydia put in.

'She often visits with her husband, Captain Flitwick — a handsome young man, but not precisely needle-witted.'

'Indeed.' John smiled at Lydia. 'You are not partial to the gentleman?'

'I must say,' Mrs Lynford admitted, 'that I thought Anthea better off for not having married him. Young girls rarely choose wisely when looks and address blind them to a man's faults.'

'And Mr Rodrigo?' Lydia could not resist asking.

'Well,' the older woman paused slightly before continuing, 'he may be a Jew, to which many parents would object, but the word about town is that he dotes on Anthea. Heaven knows he is plump in the pockets and apparently most generous. An attractive man as well, which is not necessarily to be sneezed at, if allied with discernment and taste, which Mr Rodrigo clearly possesses. All in all, I consider him definitely a cut above the good captain.'

'Have you encountered the Flitwicks since their return?' John inquired.

'They left the Pump Room only a few minutes before you arrived here.' She gave them both a knowing look. 'I have the feeling that your interest is more than idle curiosity?'

'Let us say,' John returned cautiously, 'that it is a private matter.'

'You will doubtless run into them at the concert on Wednesday night, or more probably at the subscription ball on Thursday.'

'Thank you.' Lydia nodded as they prepared to depart. 'We will remember that.'

'I wish you God speed — and good hunting!'

'A most perspicacious old lady,' John remarked as they made their way outside.

'Perhaps a little *too* knowing,' she agreed.

CHAPTER THIRTEEN: A SEEMINGLY WASTED DAY

John and Lydia continued their wanderings, ending at the Rodrigo household. Here they discovered that Anthea and Rachel were not at home, having departed to make some necessary purchases before attending the ball on Thursday night. Having ascertained as much, the couple left after assuring the housekeeper that they would rendezvous with the Rodrigos later in the day.

They returned to their lodgings, where John decided to peruse a paper which he had brought from Diddlington but had not bothered with until now when he was a little bored and restless. He read out loud some of the news which had lately been published in their own corner of the country.

'The captain of a small barge — one Ronald Rookhouse — recently fished a mermaid out of the Ouse. He bound her and held her captive for several hours, but he fell asleep and when he awakened she had disappeared and returned to her watery home.'

'Clearly,' Lydia commented, 'the man had been imbibing a little too much gin. Ten to one, he had a fine barque of frailty on board for the evening but became confused about it later.'

'This is more in your line, perhaps,' John suggested, then read out: 'A certain Edwin Chittering, manservant to a Mr and Mrs Griffen of Alfriston, has confessed to murdering his aged employers with a carving knife from their kitchen. It is,' he added, 'not very many miles from Diddlington.'

'If the man has confessed to the crime,' she said, 'there can be nothing for our purposes.'

'There seems no pleasing you this morning,' John complained. 'What about the story of Master Peter Trenton, thirteen years of age, who has disappeared from his village after telling his parents he would be visiting a friend at a nearby farm.'

'Poor child!' Lydia sighed and shook her head. 'He probably fell victim to one of the press-gangs. A sad business, but too common a practice. Very likely he is aboard one of His Majesty's frigates at this very moment.'

At length they grew bored and decided to rest before repairing to the Rodrigos later that evening.

* * *

Anthea's day was rather a vexatious one, attending to both Rachel and her friend, Sally, while they engaged in purchasing a few items they deemed absolutely necessary before any ball. Sally — whose Christian name, Susannah, had been replaced in her childhood with the apt title 'Silly Sally' — was to accompany them to the Assembly Rooms, but the poor girl was incapable of making a decision and wasted so much time on the rival merits of embroidery and lace, that Anthea began to feel a very real headache coming on.

When they at last exited the establishment, however, they were almost blocked by two ladies standing near the entrance with their backs to the trio. They were whispering and giggling so intently that they did not even notice the other three standing behind them.

'My dear,' the first lady, tall and gaunt, announced in rather stronger accents, 'you should have seen them.'

'Miss Halliwell and the Jew?' the other asked.

'Dressed in the latest of fashions, and pleased as a peacock, no doubt!' She sniffed in conscious derision. 'Well, she has got herself a rich husband, which is what matters most to her.'

'She no longer needs to steal to get on in the world,' her short, squat companion said, sneering. 'Now that she is Shylock's wife, her husband can do her thieving for her.'

'If she should ever approach me, I will know what to say to her, I can tell you!'

The two young girls felt extremely awkward, but when they glanced at Anthea they were surprised to see a decidedly militant look in her eyes. She knew these two from her younger days, when they had been envious of the popularity of the young Miss Halliwell and were now eager to vent their accumulated malice. Leaning forward, she tapped the speaker on the shoulder with one gloved finger.

'Pray, do not be shy, Mrs Wescott,' she said with cool disdain. 'If you are so certain of what you wish to say to me, by all means say it.'

'I . . . I . . . you should not be listening to the private conversation of others, ma'am!' was all that Mrs Wescott replied, flustered and ill-at-ease.

'That cannot be what you meant to say,' Anthea replied. 'Perhaps,' she added with spurious sympathy, 'you had some news concerning your uncle: the one who lives in Hampshire and is famed for frolicking about the lawn in nothing but a neck cloth and a pair of old boots. I believe they charge sixpence for visitors to come and gape at him.'

'That is a vicious rumour, which you should be ashamed to repeat.' The lady's face was scarlet, her breathing heavy with indignation.

'Truly?' Anthea feigned surprise. 'But I had it on such excellent authority. I believe that such aberrations are not always inherited, so you may be easy on that head. I wonder, though, if Miss Hammond, the young lady betrothed to your brother, is aware of it. Someone should just drop a hint in her ear, should they not?'

'You would not dare to mention such a thing!' She was caught between anger and humiliation.

Anthea gave her look for look.

'I have no intention of doing so,' she answered, unconcerned. 'I rarely whisper slanderous assertions about others, as less scrupulous persons do. There is something so ill-bred about it, is there not?'

'We will bid you good day, ma'am.' The lady's face and figure were alike rigid.

'And still you have not told me what you wished to say to me.' Anthea shook her head sadly. 'I could think of a number of things to tell you both, but I believe that the Bible warns us of casting pearls before swine. Or would that be *sows*?'

The ladies made haste to leave, and the two girls beside Anthea regarded her with something approaching awe. To tell the truth, she had been somewhat startled by her own temerity. But being loved by her husband had given her a confidence she never before possessed. What were two prating fools to her?

'Well done, Thea!' Rachel cried.

'Mrs Wescott was a spiteful wretch even when she was a mere Miss Rembert. And her companion, Miss Mellor, is a hateful crone whose grandfather was no more than a butcher in Cheapside. It is time someone set them both to the rightabouts!'

'Do tell me,' Sally begged, 'is it true that Mrs Wescott's uncle is a lunatic?'

'I have heard so these ten years and more.' Anthea walked on briskly, the other two hard-pressed to keep up with her.

'I do not think,' Rachel said with a grin, 'that those two will be likely to accept a dinner invitation from us.'

'There is no possibility of them receiving one.'

On that viperish note, they arrived home.

CHAPTER FOURTEEN: A NIGHT AT THE BALL

That evening, John and Lydia, accompanied by the Rodrigos, attended a concert in the Upper Rooms, which was about as entertaining as most such evenings were. Nothing remarkable was either heard or done, they saw nothing of the Flitwicks, and it was altogether a somewhat disappointing evening. All their hopes now centred on the ball which was to be held the following evening.

Thursday dragged by at an exceptionally slow pace, but evening found everyone dressed in their latest purchases, all finery and frippery. For Rachel it was a historic event, as she would be making her first appearance as an eligible young lady. The Bath Marriage Mart might not be as prestigious as that of London, and the Assembly Rooms, situated between Bennett and Alfred Streets, were not as exclusive as Almack's with its aristocratic patronesses, but one might make the acquaintance of any number of respectable and well-heeled gentlemen who would pass for suitable husbands.

Comfortably ensconced in a very fine hired carriage, Anthea counselled her stepdaughter not to expect a great deal from this first foray into the age-old war between the sexes.

'It is no matter that I am not a beauty like you, Thea,' Rachel assured her. 'I am an heiress, after all, and shall not want for offers.'

'So long as you do not mind allying yourself with a heartless fortune hunter,' her father quipped.

'If he be good-looking and reasonably well-bred, I shall have no cause to repine.'

'Your standards are not very high, I collect?' Anthea was not so amused.

'Where men are concerned,' the young girl answered with careless cynicism, 'it is best not to harbour unrealistic expectations.'

'I dream of wedding a handsome duke — or perhaps a marquis — who will whisk me away to his castle in a chaise-and-four!' Sally, who accompanied them, contributed with a romantic sigh.

'Most dukes and viscounts are very plain-faced, I believe,' Rachel answered, quashing her high hopes. 'And you are no prettier than I am, Sally — and not as wealthy, either — so you had best be prepared to settle for a mere Mister.'

Anthea frowned at them both. 'You had best be looking for someone whom you can hold in esteem and affection — the pair of you.'

'We cannot expect a romantic adventure such as yours, Mrs Rodrigo,' Sally was forced to admit.

'Oh, Thea will never admit that she thoroughly enjoyed her elopement, however reprehensible it may have been.'

'I hope you do not mean to suggest,' Anthea said sternly, 'that your father is not a respectable gentleman, Rachel.'

'Oh, very respectable!' She chuckled. 'Snatching his love away at dead of night and marrying her out of hand, against the wishes of her papa.'

Anthea shook her head but could not repress a smile.

'I shudder to think what a cake you will make of yourself tonight.'

'Do not fear, dearest Thea,' Rachel attempted to be serious for a moment. 'I shall be the primmest, most proper, and by far the dullest girl at the ball.'

'Forgive me if I take leave to disbelieve you.'

At least the child *looked* just as a well brought-up young lady should, Anthea thought. Their innumerable shopping expeditions had not been in vain. Rachel was not a beauty, but she had an animated countenance and a pair of sparkling dark eyes inherited from her father. Her skin was rather brown, and Anthea felt that white — though the most common colour for girls in their first season — would have made her look somewhat sallow. Instead, she had chosen a soft blue which was much more suitable.

The carriage drew up beside the colonnade at the north side of the rooms at ten minutes past seven. Alighting from it, Miss Quimby's mama, who was such a quiet and nondescript person that the others had all but forgotten her presence, began to shepherd her daughter into the building. The ball had begun at six, and there was a line of sedan chairs along the inner side against the plain stone facade of the building. Gideon offered his arm to both his daughter and his wife.

'I will be the envy of every man in the room tonight,' he exclaimed. 'To be escorting two such paragons of wit and beauty.'

'That is laying it on much too thick, Papa!'

Anthea looked at him, thinking that she would feel very proud to be entering the rooms on his arm tonight. He really was looking very handsome, at least to her eyes. His dark jacket and dark eyes and hair gave him a somewhat rakish look. It was the first time they had been to a public function since their marriage. Until now, they had kept very much to themselves, which suited Anthea. But it was inevitable that they must go out into society. She was part hope, part dread as she wondered who might give her the cut direct and how many ladies would be murmuring spiteful tattle behind their unfurled fans.

'It must be a long time since you have attended a ball,' Rachel pointed out with that penetrating look so reminiscent of her papa.

'Just so.' She drew a deep breath as they prepared to enter the ballroom. 'I trust that I have not forgotten how to conduct myself.'

'The last time you were Miss Halliwell,' Gideon squeezed her hand. 'Now you are Mrs Rodrigo.'

'I like it much better,' she told him truthfully. With him beside her, she felt she could face anything. She knew that she was looking her best in a gown of emerald green and gold silk cut low across the bosom. Quite the thing for a married lady.

Pushing through a throng of bejewelled females and severely garbed gentlemen, they made their entrance without any fanfare. Even Rachel was impressed by the room and its numerous occupants.

'It is very grand!' she exclaimed, reminding them both of how young she really was.

'A fitting stage upon which to make one's entrance into society,' Gideon agreed.

For some minutes they milled about to little purpose, lost in a sea of waving plumes where silks and satins rustled like waves upon a rocky shore. Several people whom Anthea recognized stared openly at the sight of her on Gideon's arm. They watched a handful of couples perform the minuet, which most young people scorned, while they waited for the musicians in the first-floor gallery to strike up a livelier country dance which would not be played for at least another half hour.

* * *

'There you are!'

This greeting was hallooed above the din of the music and innumerable conversations being carried on all at once. The speaker was Lydia Savidge, on the arm of her husband.

'I was wondering if we would be able to find you in this crush,' Gideon admitted as they came up to them.

'We have been here this age!' Lydia announced.

'Twenty minutes by my watch,' John corrected her and she made a face at him. How young they both were, Anthea thought: several years younger than herself, certainly. Could these two really be of any help to them?

'We are hoping that Captain Flitwick and his wife will be here,' Lydia reminded them. Anthea had all but forgotten that introducing Gideon's daughter into society was only one of the reasons for their attendance here tonight. The butterflies once more fluttered about her stomach at this realization.

'If they are not,' Gideon said, 'they must be the only residents in the town who are outside these walls.'

'Look!' Rachel cried. 'There is Sally — Miss Quimby. I thought we must have lost her.'

Sally was beside them in a matter of moments, her mama in tow. Poor Mrs Quimby muttered something unintelligible and looked remarkably like a frightened squirrel. She was woefully unsuited to the task of introducing her daughter into society but performed her duty with a grim determination to get rid of her offspring as soon as she could find a willing gentleman. More of a liability than an asset, Anthea quickly disposed of her by offering to take charge of both young ladies, while pointing out an empty seat against the wall nearby where she might enjoy a comfortable coze with an old acquaintance.

'A masterful manoeuvre, Mrs Rodrigo,' Lydia said with genuine admiration.

'You are indeed the Queen of Stepmothers,' Rachel agreed.

It was not very long before the two girls spied several eligible partners whose fathers were business associates of the Rodrigos and neighbours of the Quimby family. After assuring herself that the boys (they could hardly be termed *men*, so young and awkward as they appeared) were quite unexceptional, Anthea watched in satisfaction as her two protégées joined in the first set of country dances. Anthea and Gideon made their way to two empty chairs, followed by Lydia and John, who stayed near enough for Mrs Rodrigo to point out their quarry as soon as ever they might discover them.

For Anthea, the next half hour seemed a positive eternity, until she at last caught a glimpse of the person she had dreaded seeing. Georgina was in a gown of palest grey, adorned with silver spangles. Anthea recalled that she was now out of full mourning for her papa, who had died some eighteen months before of a sudden and violent stomach disorder. She was rather stouter than she had been and her countenance did not indicate any great degree of happiness. It was not her appearance nor her gown, however, which caused Anthea to catch her breath suddenly and instinctively clench her fingers around her husband's arm.

Around Georgina's rather short neck, reflecting the light from the chandeliers overhead, was a necklace of rubies and diamonds: the same necklace which had led to her friend's disgrace. Against the grey gown and the smooth white of its wearer's skin, the effect was truly striking.

The others followed the direction of her gaze, recognizing instantly what had caused the frozen look on Anthea's face. There was no need of further identification, for it was clear that they had at last found their target. The immediate question was how they were to deal with a situation which was so inescapably awkward.

* * *

Each of the two ladies in question bowed slightly in greeting. It was Georgina who spoke first.

'Good evening, Anthea — or should I call you Mrs Rodrigo?' Her voice was rather brittle and her smile did not reach her eyes.

'It is an age since I have seen you, Georgina,' Anthea answered, more poised than she had thought possible. 'And as we are old . . . acquaintances, there is no need for any formality between us, is there?'

'Indeed not.' She turned her gaze toward Gideon. 'And this, I take it, is your husband?'

Introductions were made all around, and Lydia and John tried to carry on a light conversation. In the resulting confusion, Anthea had barely registered the presence of Georgina's husband. But as he joined in the greetings, she was able to observe him more closely. He was as handsome as ever, though his hair was thinning slightly above his brow. He seemed strained, as if this meeting was more of a trial to him than to his wife. As for Anthea, she wondered what she could have seen in him that prompted her to accept his proposal all those years ago. He seemed oddly shabby to her now. But then she was forced to acknowledge that every man suffered in comparison to Gideon.

The Flitwicks stayed for mere minutes before dismissing themselves and pushing through the growing throng of dancers. As soon as they were gone, the two couples left behind them began to compare their impressions and discuss what strategy they might adopt.

'She clearly had heard of your marriage,' Lydia pointed out.

'And doubtless wore the necklace tonight as a kind of challenge to you, Mrs Rodrigo,' John added.

'I was quite astonished,' Anthea confessed.

'You recovered beautifully, however,' Lydia assured her.

'And what did you think of them, Gideon?' Anthea asked her husband.

'Your friend is plump and pretty in a rather common way,' he answered her slowly. 'But I suspect that she has her husband very much under her thumb. A tyrant in petticoats, Mrs Flitwick.'

'And her husband?' John queried.

'Has my sincere sympathy.'

They all gave vent to a much-needed laugh at this, before Gideon made a pronouncement which left them gaping in disbelief.

'What surprised me most of all,' he said, 'was the realization that those famous jewels of hers are paste.'

'Paste?' Anthea demanded.

'Paste?' their two friends echoed.

'I would almost be willing to stake my reputation upon it,' he said firmly. 'I wish that my friend, Mr Feingold, had been able to have a look at them. For myself, I am all but certain of it.'

'If that is true,' John returned, 'then Mrs Flitwick must be well aware of it.'

'Undoubtedly,' Gideon agreed.

'The nub of the matter, however,' Lydia added slowly, 'is how long she has been wearing this copy of her necklace. Is it something quite recent, or have the gems been false for seven years?'

'I am sure that the necklace she placed in my keeping back then was genuine,' Anthea insisted.

'And, after all,' her husband pointed out, 'the jeweller then would have undoubtedly discovered any substitution.'

'Unless,' Lydia speculated, 'he was less than honest himself.'

'As he is a good friend of mine,' Gideon answered, 'I would be willing to vouch for his character.'

'At any rate,' John said, tapping his chin with his forefinger, 'it is certainly a curious addition to the conundrum we have before us.'

CHAPTER FIFTEEN: THE BALL CONTINUES

The Rodrigos and the Savidges, having ascertained all that was likely to be of use to them for the evening, considered that they might have the pleasure of dancing before returning home for the night. While they were thus engaged, young Rachel was making a new acquaintance of some importance.

She had just finished an energetic quadrille and bade farewell to her partner, who went off in pursuit of other toes on which to tread. Sally had disappeared and Rachel decided that she had better go in search of her father and stepmother. Turning in the general direction of the spot where she had left them, she was unaware that a gentleman was standing slightly to her right and immediately behind her. He happened to be turning at precisely the same moment, and they cannoned into each other with such force that Rachel was actually knocked backward and might well have fallen had he not reached out to take hold of her.

'I beg pardon, miss,' the stranger said. 'I am a clumsy oaf, but I trust that I have done you no injury?'

'Not at all, sir,' she answered, looking up at him. 'I am quite as much at fault as you are.'

It was as well, she thought, that she was not of a romantic disposition. She might well have fallen in love at first sight with this exemplar of masculine beauty. He was tall and very handsome, with light brown hair and eyes to match. He had a fine figure too, which his formal attire displayed to advantage. She judged him to be perhaps one or two-and twenty.

'You are very generous to acquit me so easily.' His smile was as dazzling as she could have expected.

'It is amazing that more such accidents do not occur in this crowd.'

'A terrible squeeze, is it not?'

'I must confess that I am enjoying it immensely.' It was now her turn to smile. 'It is my first ball, you see.'

'I felicitate you.' He gave a slight bow, adding, 'Is it too much to expect that you might have a dance free on this momentous occasion? I assure you that I am much better at dancing than walking about.'

'But you are a complete stranger, sir,' she pointed out somewhat doubtfully. 'I am sure my stepmother would be horrified were I to stand up with you.'

'Stepmother?' he asked with ready sympathy. 'No doubt she is a dragon of a female, intent on spoiling your evening in whatever diabolical way she might contrive.'

'A dragon?' She laughed outright. 'I assure you nothing could be further from the case. She is quite delightful, much as it pains me to admit it. And a positive Diamond, who casts me quite into the shade.'

'That I do not believe.'

'Well, it is true. I am no golden goddess.'

'But you are a most charming young lady.'

'And you are a little too quick with your tongue, sir.'

'I am light on my feet as well,' he said persuasively.

'Then I will be happy to watch you dancing with some other young lady.'

It was a mild flirtation — her very first — and it seemed that she had a natural talent for it.

'You are too cruel, Fair Unknown.' His eyes sparkled with mischief. 'But there is no one about to introduce us, so

I shall perform that office myself. I am Quentin Safford, at your service!'

'Safford?' She frowned, eyeing him with sudden speculation. 'I know that I have heard that name before . . .'

'I am Lord Safford's son,' he said, striking a mock-aristocratic attitude.

'Never say that I am addressing a future viscount!' she exclaimed, suitably impressed.

'A most unlikely eventuality,' he said, depressing his own pretensions. 'I have not one but three elder brothers.'

'So you are merely *the Honourable* Quentin Safford.' She shook her head sadly. 'It is too bad, sir.'

'I know it must sink me considerably in your estimation.'

'Not at all.' She treated him to a considering glance. 'If you are a younger son, then I suppose you are hanging out for a wealthy wife?'

'Naturally,' he answered at once, clearly enjoying this unconventional conversation. 'What else is there for a younger son to do, after all?'

'Then you are in luck, sir. I,' she said grandly, 'am an heiress.'

'Are you, indeed?' His lips twitched, but he managed to maintain his gravity. 'It seems that fortune has smiled upon me this evening. Only tell me your name, that I may prostrate myself at your feet and offer my hand and heart to you at once.'

'I am Rachel Rodrigo.'

'Shall we elope tonight, Miss Rodrigo?' he inquired politely. 'Or would you prefer to wait until we know each other a little better? Tomorrow, perhaps?'

She could not stifle a giggle at this. 'It would be quite in keeping with my family, I assure you. My papa eloped with Anthea only a few weeks ago.'

'Did he so?'

'Rachel!' Anthea's voice interrupted their *tete-a-tete*. 'I was beginning to wonder whether you had fled the ballroom.'

'You must be Mrs Rodrigo, ma'am,' The Hon. Quentin Safford addressed her before Rachel could respond.

'Did I not tell you she was a Diamond?'

'You did indeed.'

Anthea looked from the gentleman to her stepdaughter, not certain whether she approved of the degree of familiarity she perceived between them.

'What scrape have you been getting into, child?' she inquired warily.

'None at all, I assure you!' Rachel protested.

'I was merely inquiring whether Miss Rodrigo might be interested in eloping with me,' Mr Safford informed her. 'I cannot allow a wealthy heiress to slip through my fingers, after all!' Anthea stared at him, comprehension and dismay dawning simultaneously.

'What dreadful things have you been saying?'

'Have I said anything dreadful, sir?' Rachel turned to the gentleman for support.

'Certainly not.' He was quick to defend her. 'Beyond informing me of your eligibility for impecunious younger sons and telling me of your papa's recent elopement with the lady who is now your stepmother, I saw nothing at all inappropriate in our conversation.'

'Good God!' Anthea cried unguardedly before addressing the man before her: 'Pray forgive her, sir. She is not quite up to snuff, you know, and . . .'

'You do not need to defend her to me, ma'am.' He bowed and smiled, and she realized that he was quite in earnest. 'I was merely desirous of dancing with the young lady, but she refused on the grounds that her cruel stepmama might not approve until we were properly introduced — which I am even now about to accomplish: The Honourable Quentin Safford at your service.'

Anthea breathed a sigh of relief. Quentin Safford might be deriving a great deal of amusement from the situation, but it was plain that he was not in the least offended at Rachel's antics. She was not personally acquainted with the family, but Lord Safford, Viscount Broadbent, was known to her by reputation. It was a fine old family with a palatial residence near Wells which had been in their possession for many generations. His interest in Rachel might be fleeting, but it was one which only a ninnyhammer would discourage. She therefore graciously consented for him to dance with her stepdaughter and watched them go through the first figures with some satisfaction. She was glad that the girl had stumbled upon someone so eligible. No doubt it would come to nothing, as such matters generally did, but it could not help but boost Rachel's self-confidence at the very least.

'Who is the young sprig dancing with Rachel?' Her husband's voice heralded his arrival just behind her.

His brows raised when Anthea informed him, but he certainly was not displeased.

'He is perfectly polite,' she added, 'and most considerate.'

'It is an acquaintance well worth encouraging,' he agreed. 'But you are not looking very happy.'

'Forgive me,' she answered. 'It has been a most eventful evening altogether, and I must confess to feeling tired and strained. Several of my old acquaintances gave me the Cut Direct.'

'It seems that neither of us will be allowed to forget the past.'

'There will always be those who will swear that I am a felon.'

'And it is unlikely,' he remarked, giving her hand a reassuring squeeze, 'that I will ever live down the fact that I am of the tribe of Israel.'

'Your heritage is something rather to be proud of,' she answered firmly. 'Were not Christ and his apostles all Jewish?'

'Well, some Christians might allow that *Judas* was Jewish. Peter and Paul — and Jesus himself — are now the property of the Gentiles, I believe. But come,' he continued. 'It is time for you to discover how well your husband dances.'

'And for you to discover how well I dance!'

He led her onto the floor, where they prepared to join the next set. He proved to be a fine dancer and partnered her through *Beechen Cliff* and *The Maid of Bath*, which reminded her of how much she had always enjoyed dancing when she was a giddy young girl. Now, of course, she need not look out for a partner. She had a husband who was always there for her. It was reassuring to realize that this was yet one more activity which they could enjoy together — though not necessarily the one they enjoyed most.

* * *

They left the floor to find Rachel and Quentin seated side by side, watching them with some interest. Rachel eagerly introduced the young man to her father.

'It is an honour,' Quentin remarked, 'to meet the intrepid Mr Rodrigo.'

'Intrepid?' Gideon seemed to think this rather amusing, if somewhat puzzling. 'I hardly think I merit such a title.'

'You are too modest, sir,' the younger man said, feigning surprise. 'Your daughter has regaled me with tales of your romantic dash to London with your beautiful bride, unperturbed by either the threats of her papa or the censure of your neighbours.'

'And at *your* age too!' Miss Rodrigo interjected, which perhaps her father did not find quite so amusing.

'I suppose I am already in my dotage,' he said.

'Nothing could be further from the case!' Anthea answered, and then blushed at what the other man might infer from that statement.

'Would it be too much to ask,' Mr Safford inquired, his lips betraying only the very slightest of twitches, 'if I might be permitted to call upon Miss Rodrigo tomorrow in Charles Street?'

'I certainly have no objection.' Gideon looked at his wife. 'Do you, my dear?'

'I am not such a fool,' she retorted tartly. 'Of course you may come to see us, sir. It seems that you are rather an *intrepid* young man yourself.'

* * *

Later that night, lying in bed with her head on her husband's shoulder, Anthea could not prevent a note of triumph from entering her comments on her stepdaughter's new beau.

'I never expected Rachel to catch the interest of such a young man at her very first public ball!'

'You have exercised a most beneficial influence upon my daughter.'

'Well, I can take no credit for tonight's work.' She shook her head. 'Rachel did absolutely nothing that I would have advised her to do. Her behaviour was quite . . . unconventional.'

'A most charitable description.'

'I am thankful that Mr Safford was amused rather than appalled.'

'I hope that you will not find your task of launching her into society too irksome, my love.'

'Not at all.' She hugged him. 'I have become very fond of Rachel. Indeed, she is like a younger sister to me.'

'As long as you do not view *me* as a father!'

'Believe me, Gideon, my feelings for you could never be described as *filial!*'

'Anthea!' He caught his breath, because she was touching him in a way which conveyed very clearly what her feelings were. 'Whatever shall I do with you?'

'Do you need me to tell you, husband?' she asked, her eyes misty with desire.

'If you will be so mischievous, perhaps I should punish you thus.' He drew her fully into his embrace and pressed a bruising kiss upon her so-willing lips.

'Such punishment,' she whispered when he allowed her to draw breath, 'is more likely to *encourage* mischief than to deter it.'

'So be it,' he replied before encouraging her even further.

For now, Rachel and Quentin were quite forgotten, along with the curious revelation of Mrs Flitwick's necklace. There would be time enough for courtship as well as for unravelling the mystery presented to them this evening. Tonight all was immersed in an ocean of supremely sweet sensation.

CHAPTER SIXTEEN: NEW FRIENDS AND OLD SINS

The Rodrigo house was a flurry of most unusual activity the following morning. First, the Honourable Quentin Safford duly presented himself. He was looking rather more than presentable in his morning coat of fawn colour, with his boots polished to perfection. His host and hostess received him with just the proper amount of attention, while Miss Rodrigo divided her attention between Quentin and Sally Quimby, who had come to vivisect every moment of the previous evening.

'I never lacked a partner,' Sally pronounced, smiling. 'I was quite fagged to death by the end of the evening.'

'What more could one ask for?' Mr Safford could not quite conceal his smile.

'He is quizzing us, Sally,' Rachel informed her friend, who otherwise would almost certainly have taken his comment at face value.

'Is he?' Miss Quimby was mystified. 'I do not see why he should.'

'He thinks himself ever so superior to flighty young ladies scarce out of the schoolroom.'

'I assure you, I do not consider myself *your* superior, Miss Rodrigo.'

'Now,' she announced, 'he will attempt a little flattery.'

'You wrong me,' the gentleman protested. 'I never use a *little* flattery, when clearly a large amount is required.'

'I think the young man has your measure, Rachel,' Anthea said.

'I think I have his as well.'

'I think,' Rachel's father looked from one to the other, 'that you are both likely to become very tiresome by and by.'

They spent a most informative morning together. By careful and unobtrusive conversation, Gideon managed to glean a few salient facts concerning the young man whose interest in his daughter was so pronounced. Quentin Safford had been in the Navy but was now employed as secretary to Lord Feversham. He had determined to study law and was perhaps inclined toward political ambitions. He had a quick wit and ready tongue which should stand him in good stead. At the same time, his manners were excellent, and he gave no indication of thinking himself above his company. On the contrary, he appeared to be well content where he was.

'We are attending a concert at Sydney Gardens this evening,' Rachel informed him. 'Shall you be there, sir?'

'I would not miss it for the world.'

'It sounds very dull,' Sally chimed in. 'I read in the *Chronicle* that there is to be a *tedium* performed, which I do not like the sound of.'

'A *tedium*?' Anthea was momentarily perplexed.

'I think,' her husband elucidated, 'that Miss Quimby means a *Te Deum*. Not that there is a great deal of difference between them.'

'Not for the listeners,' Anthea agreed.

'Pay no heed to them, Sally,' Rachel reassured her friend. 'They mean to be clever at our expense. Only see how Mr Safford grins at their jests.'

'Forgive me, Miss Rodrigo,' the gentleman apologized. 'I must admit that I have seldom seen a couple so ideally suited — or so delightful — as your father and stepmother.'

'Now you flatter even my family!' she exclaimed.

'And quite put us to the blush.' Anthea really did colour slightly, eyeing him with increased speculation.

'I cry pardon, ma'am.' He bowed in mock obeisance. 'I hope that my idle remarks will not result in my banishment from your home.'

'I suppose we shall be lax enough to permit your return.'

He departed a few minutes later, having timed the length of his visit to perfection. Any shorter, and it would have seemed as if only a sense of duty had constrained him to call upon them at all, and a lengthier visit might have been considered pushing and ill-bred.

* * *

Hardly did the young ladies have time to bemoan his absence and retreat to Rachel's bedchamber for a more comfortable coze, when yet another arrival was heralded. This time it was not a handsome young man, but two ladies and a large gentleman. In fact, it was Lydia and John, accompanied by Mrs Lynford, their acquaintance from the Pump Room, whom they encountered on the doorstep of the Rodrigo residence.

Anthea was surprised but genuinely happy to greet the older woman, whom she had not seen for so long. She introduced her to Gideon and then they all seated themselves in preparation for a conversation which, although they did not know it, was about to take an unexpected turn.

'You are looking as radiant as you did seven years ago,' Mrs Lynford exclaimed in genuine admiration. 'Marriage must agree with you.'

'Well, my husband certainly agrees with me.'

'Thank you, my dear,' Gideon replied.

'And your young friends,' Mrs Lynford continued with a glance toward John and Lydia, 'are quite modish and remarkably astute, I would say.'

'Being young and being foolish are not necessarily one and the same,' John reminded her.

'I am sure that you encountered Captain Flitwick and his wife yesterday evening at the ball.'

'I would say,' Lydia interjected, with a knowing look, 'that Mrs Flitwick made it her business to meet you, Anthea.'

'Wearing those jewels on purpose to discompose you, no doubt.' Mrs Lynford gave a snort of contempt.

'A gesture both spiteful and ill-bred,' Gideon concluded.

'And not as effective as she might have wished.' This was John's contribution. 'You behaved with admirable composure, ma'am.'

'Thank you,' Anthea said. 'I assure you that I was quite as perturbed as she could have wished, even if I did not show it.'

'I know I will seem like an old tabby,' Mrs Lynford confessed, 'but I own that I never liked the girl. From the moment that she came out, she adopted airs which were much too lofty for the daughter of a tradesman. Modesty was certainly not her forte.'

'Had my father not been a peer,' Anthea admitted, 'I have sometimes wondered whether she would have befriended me at all.'

'She strikes me as the very image of Mrs Elton,' Lydia agreed.

'Who is Mrs Elton?' They all demanded an explanation, which Lydia provided.

'She is a character in a most deliciously naughty comic novel, called *Emma*. Alas, there are far too many like her.'

'I really did try to feel some sympathy for her when her necklace went missing,' Mrs Lynford said, remembering the incident. 'Especially so, when her own maid disappeared at almost the same time. It was rumoured that she had run off with a handsome young footman from the house next door to them.'

'I did not know of that,' Anthea admitted. 'I was lost in my own problems, of course.'

'You can scarcely be blamed for that!'

Lydia and John exchanged a significant glance before the former proceeded to question the old lady further.

'Her maid disappeared, you say?'

'Indeed. It was a minor scandal, but quite eclipsed by the affair of the necklace.'

'Do you recall the name of the maid and what she looked like?'

All eyes now turned to Lydia. What, they wondered, was this young lady about?

'Let me see.' Mrs Lynford screwed up her face in an effort of concentration, before speaking slowly and carefully: 'She was a rather tall girl, with lovely blonde hair. Her name was — it is quite on the tip of my tongue — I think it was . . . Nancy. Yes, that was it.'

'Would you say,' John continued the interrogation, 'that this Nancy bore some slight resemblance to Mrs Rodrigo?'

Mrs Lynford was quite taken aback.

'I suppose,' she answered, 'that if she were fashionably dressed, and in a dimly lit room, she might pass for Anthea.'

They all paused for a moment before Gideon addressed the younger man.

'What are you suggesting, John?'

'Seven years ago,' he began suggestively, 'a tall blonde lady, heavily veiled, appeared with a stolen necklace which she wished to sell to whatever unscrupulous person might be interested. It was not Anthea, but neither was it a phantom.'

'You believe that Georgina's maid may have been involved?' Anthea asked.

'Well,' Lydia responded, 'it strikes me as a little too much of a coincidence that she conveniently disappeared shortly afterward, putting her out of the way of any suspicion.'

'But if she ran away with the footman—'

'That, as you say, ma'am, was merely a rumour.'

'Which,' Lydia said, 'could well have been started by Georgina herself. I should not be at all surprised if it were so.'

'It is very easily done,' Mrs Lynford acknowledged. 'A whisper that a friend of a friend has a servant who had seen the footman and Nancy together . . . and suddenly everyone is saying that they were having secret trysts at midnight.'

'It is too fantastic.' Anthea shook her head, unwilling to accept this promising theory.

'Perhaps,' Mrs Lynford replied. 'But I certainly would not put it past your old friend. She is cunning, that one. Of that I am quite certain.'

* * *

She left the matter there, and made her exit only a few minutes later, with a promise to call upon them again in the near future. After her departure, there was a moment of silence as each of them sought to collect their thoughts.

'Do you think,' Lydia ventured at last, 'that the Flitwicks are likely to attend the concert in Sydney Gardens this evening?'

'We can hardly accost them and demand to know the whereabouts of a maid the lady employed seven years ago!' Gideon chuckled softly. 'I think we would have a cold reception.'

'One has to be a little more circumspect than that,' Lydia agreed. 'I will hint to Mrs Flitwick that I am rather suspicious of Anthea, and then express my sympathy for all that she suffered, adding that I had heard her maid absconded with the butler next door.'

'He was a footman, I believe Mrs Lynford said,' Anthea corrected her.

'Just so.' John gave a boyish grin. 'That will prompt the lady to correct my wife and perhaps provide more extensive information which might or might not be useful.'

'It seems that you are a rather cunning pair yourselves!'

'This is not our first experience with malefactors of various kinds.'

'Previously,' John put in, 'we have more or less stumbled upon various crimes — usually of the murderous variety. But in this case we were summoned by yourself to right a most serious wrong.'

'And this,' his wife added, 'is the first time that we have learned something which may well be the key to the entire puzzle.'

'It hardly seems so,' Anthea answered doubtfully.

'Then again,' Gideon said, more optimistically, 'things which appear as trifles may be more significant than we imagine.'

'Very true.' John nodded seriously. 'By pulling at one small thread, an entire coat may come unravelled!'

CHAPTER SEVENTEEN:
A MOST EVENTFUL CONCERT

The concert was everything they had anticipated, and the *Te Deum* all that Miss Quimby had dreaded. A semi-circular projection from the main Sydney Hotel formed a place for the orchestra, with the musicians looking down upon the patrons who milled about at their leisure. Nobody actually paid much attention to the music, despite the skill of the performers. At 9.30 p.m. their boredom was relieved by a grand display of fireworks, crackling and sparkling above the gardens while the crowd below gasped and applauded at appropriate intervals.

In the midst of the pyrotechnics, the two younger ladies managed to become separated from their chaperons. Quentin, however, kept a watchful eye on both Rachel and Sally. He observed Miss Quimby desert her friend momentarily and attach herself with dogged determination to a young gentleman for whom she had obviously conceived a violent tendre, but who clearly did not reciprocate her interest. From where he stood, the young man appeared absolutely terrified by her lovelorn antics.

'A most energetic performance,' he commented aloud, coming up beside Rachel and following the direction of her gaze.

'Poor Sally!' she exclaimed with a chuckle. 'She may be wasting her time, but has provided me with the finest entertainment I have witnessed this evening.'

'You did not enjoy the music?' He smiled down at her.

'Quite as well as I expected to,' she answered. 'I confess that I prefer to hear Anthea on the pianoforte. She is a very fine player.'

'It is plain that your father dotes upon her,' he remarked.

'Hopelessly besotted,' she said bluntly. 'To be honest, Papa has had a tendre for her from the moment he met her some five years ago. He was recently widowed then, but you know his marriage to my mama was not a love match but made up between their parents. I have certainly never seen him look at any woman the way he looks at Anthea.'

'I would say that she is as much in love as he is,' Safford suggested.

'I do believe that she is,' Rachel paused, giving the matter some thought. 'I do not doubt that it will not be very long before she is increasing . . . What is it, Mr Safford?'

Poor Quentin was almost in whoops at this artless comment.

'Nothing at all, Miss Rodrigo,' he answered.

At this moment they were joined by Anthea, who had been looking for Rachel for several minutes while Gideon went in search of refreshments.

'Where on earth have you been, child?' she asked her stepdaughter. 'And what dreadful things have you been saying to this gentleman?'

'I have said nothing dreadful,' she protested. 'Have I done so, Mr Safford?'

'Oh, nothing at all, I assure you, ma'am.' He caught his lips between his teeth before continuing, 'Miss Rodrigo was merely speculating on how soon you would be — how did you put it? — increasing.'

'What!'

'Well,' the young lady added, 'considering how frequently you and Papa seem to be copulating, it surely cannot be very long!'

Anthea was rendered completely speechless by this statement and looked rather like Lot's wife: a pillar of salt.

Mr Safford, meanwhile, could no longer contain his mirth, and was forced to put a hand over his mouth to stifle a burst of unseemly laughter. Rachel, he thought, was a source of never-failing delight! He was quite bewitched by her curious ignorance of social conventions and her innate honesty which rolled over polite hypocrisy and left it floundering in her wake.

'I shall die,' Anthea announced, finding her voice at last, 'of mortification!'

'Have I not the correct word?' Rachel seemed more concerned for her vocabulary than her reputation.

'I would say that the word was exactly right, Miss Rodrigo.' Turning to Anthea, he added, 'And surely, ma'am, there is no record of someone actually expiring from mortification?'

'Then you may congratulate me on being the first,' she snapped. 'How can you encourage her in such . . . such profligacy, sir?'

The situation, in her opinion, had gone from bad to worse with alarming swiftness.

'I beg pardon, Mrs Rodrigo,' he said, trying to sound more contrite than he felt. He had a pronounced and perhaps rather wicked sense of humour, and these two ladies were providing him more than the usual cause for mirth.

'Do you and Papa not cop—?'

'Rachel!' Anthea cut short her speech with more severity than she had ever employed with her before. 'If you repeat that word once more, I shall have a fit of strong hysterics right here in Sydney Gardens!'

'I'm sorry, Thea.' At least *her* contrition was genuine, Anthea thought, although she still had no idea of what she was guilty.

'Where did you learn such an offensive word?'

'From Shakespeare,' the younger girl announced proudly. '*King Lear*, to be precise. Papa,' she explained, 'has a very old folio copy of many of the plays, and I have read them all.'

'Shakespeare,' Anthea spoke with considerable opprobrium, 'may have been a great writer, but there are times when I could wish that he had been born a rat and a cat had eaten him.'

'But the sins of the Bard should not be visited upon his readers, should they?' Quentin protested.

Anthea ignored his remark and continued to address herself to Rachel.

'Have you any idea what the word means?' she demanded.

'Papa explained it to me,' she retorted, then added conscientiously, 'although not in any detail. He merely said that it is what a man and woman do when they are married, and it is how the human race is propagated. I do not believe, however, that marriage is always necessary.'

'It seems that your husband is responsible for his daughter's moral turpitude, Mrs Rodrigo,' Quentin said with deliberate provocation.

'He certainly has a great deal to answer for.'

'Perhaps Mr Rodrigo should have told his child that babies come down from Heaven on the wings of angels, or some such thing.'

'No.' Anthea's rejection of this was grudging but sincere. 'It is not good to tell untruths to children, I think. But he might be a little more circumspect in what he allows his daughter to read.'

'I often wonder,' he answered, 'what most young ladies feel on their wedding night. Unless they have helped bathe their younger brothers, the sight of a certain portion of the male anatomy and the realization of the function it performs, must come as quite a shock.'

'Not as great a shock as one might think.' She blushed in the semi-darkness. 'We quickly learn to appreciate it, I assure you.'

'Indeed.' He could barely repress another laugh. What next would these remarkable women say? 'But it is something one should be ashamed to discuss openly.'

'Not ashamed,' she corrected in all seriousness. 'Not everything that is hidden is shameful. Men draw a veil over many things because they are sacred. That which becomes too familiar is often dismissed as of little value.'

'A wise observation, ma'am.'

'Anyone who takes Anthea for a fool,' Rachel chimed in, 'is sadly mistaken. But I will promise to be more cautious in my speech. I do not wish to incur your censure, Thea.'

'It is not *my* censure you should fear.' Anthea sighed. 'The world has little use for artlessness and honesty, my dear. The one man who made the outrageous claim to *be* the truth was crucified by the world, which moved on, not realizing that something had been set in motion that would change it for ever.'

'It has been a most enlightening evening,' the gentleman said.

'I am grateful that we have not offended you,' Anthea told him with real gratitude. 'Some men would not be so kind.'

'Any man who cannot appreciate the Rodrigo women must be a sad bore, and too stiff-rumped to be of use to anyone.'

He glanced down at Rachel, realizing that he was completely entranced by her refreshing lack of airs and graces. Mr and Mrs Rodrigo certainly had their hands full with this precocious baggage of a girl — and he fully hoped to have his arms full of her in due course, for he was a man of decision and had quite made up his mind that he had found the young woman who would be the perfect wife for him. Whether she had any inkling of this, he was not so certain, but in time he was confident that she would come to see what was already plain to him. His family might not relish the connection. However, being a younger son, they would not be overly critical as they would with their heir. Besides, her father was a man of considerable wealth, and money (if there was enough of it) could cover even the stain of his deplorable ancestry.

Gideon Rodrigo appeared to be a man of taste as well as enterprise, and Quentin was happy to know that he truly liked and admired his future father-in-law. Anthea Rodrigo was a woman of birth, breeding, and rare beauty. It was clear that this couple was very much in love. He would have no hesitation in allying himself to a family which he found very much to his liking. It was fortunate that he had chosen to visit Bath, and he judged that his visit might be rather longer than originally intended.

* * *

It was at this juncture that Gideon appeared with a glass of negus for Anthea, and one for himself. Immediately behind him came John and Lydia Savidge, who arrived fresh from a brief interview with the Flitwicks.

'Have you learned anything more?' Gideon inquired hopefully.

John shook his head, while Lydia pursed her lips and looked anything but happy.

'The lady was not very forthcoming,' John said eventually.

'She repeated the story of her maid absconding with the footman,' Lydia said. 'But it sounded a little too much like something she had learned by rote and could rattle off without even thinking.'

'You think she is lying?'

'I would almost be willing to wager a considerable sum on that assumption, Anthea.'

'The girl might have participated in the scheme, pre-tended to be me.' Anthea's brow puckered slightly as she concentrated on this rank speculation. 'She would have been paid handsomely to keep her mouth shut on that head.'

'Or . . .' Lydia paused and was quickly halted by her husband.

'I know precisely where this is headed, my dear.'

'Do you?' She did not look too pleased by this.

'Must you suspect a murderer behind every bush?'

'Murderer!' the other four listeners cried in chorus.

'I fear that I am quite in the dark,' Quentin Safford put in, genuinely surprised. 'Are you on the hunt for a killer among us?'

'I have said too much, I fear,' John apologized.

'Not at all,' Anthea assured him. 'I quite look upon Quentin as one of the family. He has already seen and heard enough that this is unlikely to come as a shock.'

'I do hope, however,' Gideon said seriously, 'that this will go no further.'

'No one shall hear anything from me.' The younger man was eager to prove his worth.

The others quickly related the bare essentials of Anthea's problem and the quest upon which they were embarked. He raised a brow but expressed his opinion that no one who knew Mrs Rodrigo could ever believe her guilty of such a crime.

'But why bring up the subject of murder?' Rachel asked. 'Surely no one has ever hinted at such a thing before.'

'My wife,' John informed them, 'has a natural predilection for the more sordid and spectacular of crimes.'

'Well, thus far it has been our general field of expertise,' she reminded him with a saucy look.

'But there is no basis for such a conjecture in this case.'

'Oh, I do not know,' Quentin answered, giving the matter some consideration. 'You mentioned that the maid may have been paid to participate in the scheme. But what if she thought she had not been paid enough?'

'What,' Lydia pounced on this with the alacrity of a dog at a particularly delicious bone, 'what if she was as greedy as Miss Shields was unscrupulous?'

'A little blackmail, you are thinking?' John wondered aloud. 'There is that possibility, of course.'

'As long as the maid was alive, Georgina could never really feel safe.' Anthea's eyes opened wide as she realized what they were all thinking. 'Surely Georgina could not be as wicked as that!'

'You would be surprised,' Lydia corrected her, 'at how wicked even the most innocent-seeming man or woman can be. At least,' she added, 'that has been our experience.'

'But we have absolutely no evidence for this.' John seemed determined to depress such pretensions before they could blossom into fixed prejudices.

'What,' Gideon asked, 'became of the footman?'

'Now that,' John smiled approvingly at him, 'is a most relevant question, the answer to which may be quite enlightening.'

'Who was his employer?' Quentin asked Anthea.

'I do not know,' she admitted with reluctance. 'This is the first I ever heard of this supposed elopement. Remember that I was a virtual recluse these last seven years. Until very recently, I scarcely knew what was going on outside the walls of my father's house, except for what I read in the *Chronicle*.'

'I saw at least one person give you the Cut Sublime this evening,' Rachel commented to her. 'We absolutely *must* clear your name, Thea!'

'We have precious little on which to base any theory of what might have happened or who might be implicated in this.'

'Well, first things first,' Lydia said, apparently more confident than the rest of them. 'I think we must consult Mrs Lynford once more. She seems to possess a wealth of information on the subject.'

'She will certainly know the identity of the young man in this drama, or at least his employer.' John seemed even more confident now than his wife.

'In the meantime,' Rachel said, turning the subject, 'I believe there is to be one more display of fireworks.'

* * *

While the rest of the party walked forward to catch a last glimpse of the fireworks, which almost immediately began exploding above them in cascades of rainbow-coloured light, Gideon and Anthea moved in the other direction, into a slightly more private part of the gardens. While all other eyes were looking upward, on impulse Gideon drew Anthea behind a conveniently placed tree and stole one quick but heated kiss.

'Let us go home now, Gideon,' she said when he released her. 'I want so much to be alone with you!'

'I am entirely of one mind with you, my wanton wife.'

'Papa!' Rachel's voice broke the enchanted moment. 'I am horrified!'

'What is it, child?' her father demanded.

'You were hugging and kissing Anthea,' she objected.

'Heavens!' Anthea exclaimed. 'So you were — and without any thought for our reputations, which must now be beyond mending.'

'It simply is not done, ma'am,' Quentin added, with mock solemnity. 'I am astonished at such flagrant debauchery.'

'I have no defence, save for the fact that my wife is so eminently kissable,' Gideon answered. 'Still, to be kissing her in public is most reprehensible. If she were my mistress, now, it would be another matter altogether.'

'Why is it,' Anthea complained, 'that a mistress always has so much more enjoyment than a wife?'

'Enjoyment is the sole purpose of keeping a mistress, is it not?'

'You are incorrigible, Papa!' His daughter shook her head.

'What is it,' Anthea pondered rhetorically, 'that the Scriptures say about taking the beam out of one's own eye before examining the mote in that of others?'

'Is that directed at me, for my earlier remarks?' Rachel demanded.

'What remarks are those?' Gideon asked, pardonably mystified.

'I have a few things to say to you about that later.' His wife gave him a direct look.

'You have a great deal to answer for in the conduct of your daughter, sir!' Quentin assumed an air of prim disapproval. 'Quite shocking, I call it.'

Rachel sniffed at this. 'You are all against me. I shall say no more.'

'Mr Safford,' Gideon said, 'I salute you. I have never known anyone who has been able to silence my daughter so effectively.'

'Well,' said John with a satirical gleam in his eye, 'I will leave you to your revels. We shall visit Mrs Lynford on the morrow and reconnoitre with you later in the day.'

'Try not to create any more scandals until then,' Lydia teased, before they disappeared amid the throng slowly exiting the gardens.

CHAPTER EIGHTEEN: PORTRAITS AND PUZZLES

The very next morning, Rachel accompanied Anthea to Milsom Street, to the studio of Mr Charles Jagger. It was her final sitting for a miniature which Gideon had insisted upon commissioning at what Anthea considered the exorbitant rate of thirty guineas. She hoped that the quality of the work would justify such extravagance.

Mr Jagger greeted them cordially and got to work almost at once. Anthea tried to compose herself while Rachel looked through the window at the pedestrians passing to and fro outside. For some time silence reigned while Anthea barely resisted the impulse to fidget. It was not many minutes, however, before the painter declared that he was finished. In fact, he said, only a few minor details had to be completed before he could deliver the portrait to Gideon within the next two days. As the two ladies were preparing to depart, however, he turned to his sitter.

'I understand,' he said, 'that the Jews are raising money to build a synagogue in Bath.'

'Are they?' Her interest was caught at once. 'I must let my husband know, if he does not already.'

'But we are Christians,' Rachel reminded her. 'It can be of no real importance to us.'

'I disagree.' Anthea shook her head. 'The Jews are as much God's people as we are. It behoves us to help them in any way we can.' She turned back to the painter. 'Thank you for telling me of this, sir.'

As they took their leave, Rachel paused a moment to warn her stepmother.

'I hope you will not go about suggesting to our acquaintances that they should contribute to the building of a synagogue here. It will only set people's backs up.'

'Do you think it would lead to problems for you and Gideon?' Anthea asked, adding somewhat hesitantly, 'It cannot be easy for you in a society which looks on you with constant suspicion. I know something of what you must feel.'

'One becomes accustomed to a certain — guarded — attitude, even from the most well-intentioned persons.' Rachel shrugged. 'It is not always comfortable, though we have not experienced anything like the persecution which our people suffer in other countries.'

'Still,' Anthea suggested, 'it might be better to remain silent this time?'

'Not,' Rachel responded, 'if you are silent from fear.'

'I am not afraid, nor ashamed,' Anthea assured her. 'People may make one feel intimidated, but I have found that they have no power to make one feel inferior.'

'Do what you think best.' Rachel smiled. 'You are not likely to be met with more than stares of astonishment.'

'I am sure they would expect no less from a woman who is so ill-bred as to be found kissing her husband in public!'

Rachel sighed in defeat. 'Well, if you will not be serious . . .'

* * *

While the two of them were taking a casual stroll back to the house, Lydia and John were visiting Mrs Lynford. Although the older woman had no more to tell them herself regarding the crime committed seven years past, she was able to assure them that the man they wanted to speak to was still residing adjacent to the house formerly belonging to Mr Shields and now the property of the Flitwicks. He might be able to tell them more concerning the elopement of his footman with the young maid. His name, she informed them, was Mr Tremblay, a gouty septuagenarian.

Calling at his residence, they were met with some surprise at the door and told that Mr Tremblay was not at home, but at the Queen's Bath, where he frequently repaired for the healing benefits of the waters which had brought fame to the town since the days of ancient Rome.

Slightly crestfallen at missing him, they almost turned away before the servant who had greeted them offered a word of encouragement: the gentleman was almost always home in the afternoon, if they wished to call again. It seemed that he had relatively few friends and would welcome a visit from almost anyone.

'I had been on the point of telling you that we must repair to the baths ourselves,' Lydia said to her husband, 'that we might snatch a bit of conversation with him.'

'That is one hardship, at least, that we need not endure.'

'You might find a dip in the baths very pleasant,' she countered.

He did not seem convinced.

'While I enjoy a warm bath as much as anyone,' John said, 'I do not think that we are yet at the age to be soaking in noxious-smelling water for the benefit of our health.'

Lydia agreed, and they returned to their lodgings for several hours before venturing out again to discover whether the old man would prove to be of use in their investigations. When they at last knocked at the gentleman's door for the second time that day, they were most graciously ushered into a neat and well-appointed parlour, where Mr Tremblay sat with his left leg resting on a small stool. He began to apologize for not rising to greet them but was forestalled by John.

'It is we who should apologize to you, sir,' the younger man said with his usual deliberation. 'It might seem much too pushing for two complete strangers to accost you when you are no doubt trying to rest.'

'Not at all, not at all, Mr Savidge,' the old man answered, and motioned toward two chairs which faced his own at a small distance. 'It is a rare treat for me to entertain anyone these days. So many of my own generation have gone on to their rewards, and the young people have no interest in someone as ancient as myself.'

'Well,' Lydia seated herself and leaned forward a little, 'we are here at the request of a friend. He is trying to find someone who disappeared about seven years ago.'

'Disappeared?' Tremblay was clearly astonished. 'I never heard of such a thing, and I cannot see how I could possibly be of help to you.'

'Do you recall,' John began as gently as possible, 'a young maid who was employed by the Shields family who resided next door?'

'We have been told,' Lydia added helpfully, 'that she was being . . . courted by a footman in your own employment.'

'Ah!' He leaned back in his chair and his eyes focused on the opposite wall as if viewing a painting from a distance. 'Now I do recall the girl you are speaking of. Nancy, I think her name was. Tall and blonde, with bright blue eyes. Lovely thing, in a slightly common way.'

'It's said,' John pressed the story to its end, 'that she eloped with the footman.'

'Yes,' the old man nodded. 'That was the general opinion, and I believed it myself for some years — for it is certain that they both quit Bath most inexplicably at about the same time.'

Lydia and John exchanged speaking glances.

'But you no longer believe it?' Lydia inquired.

'I know it to be false,' he said with complete confidence.

'How so?' John asked him in surprise.

'It is a strange coincidence, I suppose,' he explained, 'but I was visiting a friend in Sussex some — let me see — some three years ago, and met up with my former footman, who had left me without so much as a note of apology.'

'In Sussex?' the two younger people asked in unison.

'Yes,' he confirmed. 'I was quite taken aback, and not best pleased.'

Both men had recognized each other at once, though Mr Tremblay admitted that he could not remember his former servant's name. The man told him that he had come into a small inheritance which had to be claimed immediately, and begged pardon for not having given proper notice. The inheritance proved to be even less than the young footman had supposed, and he had gone into service with an elderly couple in Sussex where he was then living.

'I actually asked him about Nancy,' Mr Tremblay told them. 'He said that it was a mere rumour, and that he had only the briefest of flirtations with the girl before quitting town. He was a handsome fellow, very popular with the girls of his own class. I fancy he had a penchant for gaming, however.'

'He had no idea where Nancy might be?' John demanded.

'None, Mr Savidge.'

'How vexatious!' Lydia exclaimed, quite put out.

'I warned you that I would be of little or no use to you!'

'So you did,' she replied more calmly. 'But that is hardly your fault, sir.'

'I wish I could help,' he replied somewhat wistfully.

'And you still cannot remember the name of your former servant?' John asked.

'I believe his Christian name was Edmund or Edwin.' He rubbed his chin, which must have helped to dislodge some scrap of memory, for he suddenly added: 'His surname was Chatsworth or Chatterley or Chadwick, or something like it . . . No, I'm afraid it escapes me for the moment.'

'If you should remember,' John said, 'please contact us as soon as you are able.'

After receiving his promise to inform them if he recalled the name, Lydia and John thanked him for his time and effort, however ineffectual, and made their exit. Neither was feeling especially clever or successful, and it seemed that they had reached the end of the road in their search for some morsel of information that might provide a clue to the mystery — if mystery it could be called.

'We have a necklace which is not what it should be.' Lydia held up her finger to indicate one item worthy of consideration.

'And,' John continued, holding up two fingers, 'we have a missing maid who did not, in fact, elope with the neighbour's footman.'

'What we do not have,' his wife concluded, 'is a shred of evidence that those two facts are connected, and no clue what became of either the real necklace or the maid!'

'And yet,' John clenched his fist as if about to plant a facer into their unseen opponent, 'I am plagued by the thought that there is something I should know — a tiny alarm bell ringing in my mind, but I cannot quite grasp what it is that I am missing.'

'Then it is best to think on something else,' she advised. 'The very effort of concentration will block your mental faculties. Let us pay a visit to the Rodrigos and tell them what we have learned.'

'Or,' John said glumly, 'what we have *not* learned.'

'I must confess,' Lydia remarked as they made their way slowly to King Street, 'that Anthea and Gideon are the only pair of lovers I have yet encountered whom I find charming rather than irritating.'

'That is because, although they are very much in love, they are able to laugh at themselves.' John paused as they turned a corner and gave a friendly nod to an elderly couple passing in the opposite direction. 'While their love is strong, they wear it lightly and can enjoy it without appearing too cloying.'

'It is a great mistake to take oneself too seriously.' Lydia smiled.

'The person who cannot bear to be laughed at is invariably a great bore.'

'And alas, a bore is incapable of seeing the truth about himself.'

'That, I fear,' John said with resignation, 'is true of everyone.'

* * *

Arriving at the Rodrigo residence, they were met by Anthea and Rachel, who listened attentively to what they had discovered from Mr Tremblay. The consensus among them was that it seemed only to muddy the waters and bring them no closer to a solution to their problem.

'But who could have started the rumour of an elopement?' Rachel asked at length.

'I believe that we were correct in our surmise,' Lydia answered, 'and that the most likely person would surely have been Georgina herself.'

'But why?'

'My dear child,' Lydia said, for all the world as if she were a wizened old woman, 'there might be several reasons.'

'First,' John added, 'if she had replaced the real jewels with paste, she would not have wanted to draw attention to the fact.'

'She might also have paid off the maid to keep her quiet, or perhaps even . . .'

'Yes?' Her husband inquired as her voice trailed off suggestively.

'I still hold that she might have been done away with if she chanced to know too much.'

'You really think that Georgina murdered her, then?' Anthea seemed determined not to entertain the thought.

'As I mentioned at the concert, my wife has a nose for murder,' John admitted somewhat ruefully.

'But Georgina, as you have seen, is quite a short girl, while Nancy was more statuesque.' Anthea remained unconvinced. 'How can she possibly have overpowered the girl and disposed of the body in the middle of Bath?'

'In the first place,' Lydia explained, 'we cannot know where the murder occurred . . .'

'Assuming that it *did* occur,' John said. 'But if Lydia's theory is correct, then it may be that Mrs Flitwick had an accomplice.'

'I had not thought of that,' Rachel admitted.

'If only we could find the footman whose name Mr Tremblay could not remember.'

'I fear that it is hopeless, Mrs Savidge.' Anthea gave a sigh of resignation.

'Nonsense!' Lydia contradicted her. 'In our experience, something always turns up which leads us to the solution and the capture of the criminal.'

'It is still hard for me to believe that my old friend could be so diabolical.'

'I suspect that she was in love with Captain Flitwick, and a woman in love is capable of anything.'

'Perhaps,' Anthea admitted with some reluctance. 'But though I can imagine myself doing many things for love of Gideon, murder is definitely not one of them.'

CHAPTER NINETEEN: DINNER AND DRAMA

The Guzmans arrived in Bath for a short stay, and Anthea conceived the notion of a dinner party with a little dancing for the younger generation. In this way, she might get to know Gideon's friends, including some of the Jewish community in Bath. In addition, she would invite Quentin Safford and Mrs Lynford. The former was one whose diplomacy she could count on and whose interest in Rachel she certainly wished to encourage. The latter was someone whose breeding and good nature would help to calm troubled social waters.

It was a relatively small gathering of not more than twenty persons, most of whom were acquainted with one another. Surveying the dining room before the arrival of her guests, she was pleased with the arrangement of the table — the new Wedgwood service neatly laid out and flanked by sparkling glassware, and silverware with fashionable, green-stained ivory handles.

'Do you think it will serve?' she asked Gideon, standing beside her.

'It looks just as it should.' He adjusted the placement of a spoon unnecessarily. 'Not that anyone is likely to notice.'

'Why not?' she demanded, slightly put out of counte-nance at the thought that all her efforts might be wasted.

'Everyone will be far too busy looking at you, my love.' He surveyed her with evident appreciation. 'You are absolutely ravishing, you know.'

She did not know, in fact, but nor did she in the least mind having it pointed out to her by the person she most desired to impress.

'Since my gown cost you a good deal of blunt, sir,' she said, splaying her skirt and striking an attitude, 'who else but you should enjoy the sight of it? Indeed, I am almost entirely your creation!'

He shook his head. 'I cannot take credit for God's handiwork, sweetheart. It is the woman, not the gown, which arouses my . . . admiration.'

'Is that what I see in your eyes?' she quizzed him boldly. 'Admiration?'

'Among other things.' His gaze was smouldering, his breath a little ragged.

'Oh Gideon,' she said, gently stroking his cheek with one hand, 'I do love you so much!'

'My dearest love,' he said thickly, pulling her against him.

'Anthea, it is too bad!'

This interruption was provided by Lavinia Guzman, who was descending the stairs along with her husband and Rachel.

'What is too bad?' Anthea queried, stepping away from Gideon.

'You will make the rest of us look hopelessly dowdy!'

'Shall I change, perhaps?'

'It would make no difference.' Rachel, as usual, did not mince matters. 'We cannot hope to compare with you and must simply make the most of such assets as we possess.'

'Well,' Anthea remarked, looking at her gown of cream-coloured muslin, 'you are certainly young enough and vivacious enough to hold your own against old married ladies like ourselves.'

The guests began to arrive soon after, and the rooms were growing quite noisy enough. She had never before hosted such a gathering, but Gideon's support could see her through any challenge life might throw in her way.

Dinner was certainly an interesting affair. One of Gideon's old friends, a Mr Shalmar, was nearest to her at her left hand, and she enjoyed a spirited discussion with him on the subject of religion. He was neither a Christian nor a Deist, but she could not think him quite respectable. He seemed to place all religions on an equal footing, which Anthea thought absurd.

'Are not religions like flowers in a field?' He cocked his head, inviting a negative response. 'One chooses the ones which are most pleasant, casting aside those which do not suit one's taste.'

'A clever analogy,' she agreed, 'but quite misleading.'

'How so?'

'Rather than flowers in a field,' Anthea suggested, 'religions are more like mushrooms in a forest. If one is going to taste them, one had better not choose those which appear most pleasing. The consequences could be deadly.'

* * *

Once the meal was over, the young people — all, with the exception of Rachel, the offspring of Gideon's friends — cajoled Anthea into playing a few dances upon the pianoforte (yet another gift from her doting husband). It was a brief, impromptu romp with much breathless laughter punctuating the country dances as they twirled about at one end of the room.

'Mrs Rodrigo plays delightfully,' Quentin said.

'She is a woman of many talents,' Gideon agreed.

'I understand,' Mr Shalmar commented, 'that she has persuaded you to contribute to the building of a synagogue here in Bath?'

'I sometimes think that she is a better Jew than I ever was.' His eyes were fixed upon his wife. 'She has been try- ing to persuade Mr Joseph to teach her Hebrew and was quite upset when he informed her that he accepted only male pupils.'

'Why would she want to learn Hebrew?' Lavinia asked in surprise.

'She wishes to prepare future generations for the day when Israel will once again become a sovereign nation.'

There was a moment of stunned silence, followed by an outburst of laughter. A moment later Anthea halted the dancing by getting up from her instrument and telling the young people that she was neglecting the rest of her guests. They accepted her decision with ill grace and sought refuge in a game of charades.

The Honourable Mr Safford was summoned by Rachel to join the youngsters. Though a little older and more serious, his quick wit was definitely wanted among the players, and Anthea suspected that her stepdaughter was vexed that he had refused to join them in the dancing.

There were other matters which occupied the minds of the adults present as well. As generally happens, the gentlemen and ladies formed themselves into two distinct camps. The men became engaged in a fierce discussion on the likelihood of survival for the new nation of Argentina, while the women debated the rival merits of the latest books, some favouring Moore's *Lalla Rookh* and others insisting on Scott's *Guy Mannering*.

* * *

Later that night, after the guests had all gone — with the exception of the Guzmans, of course, who were staying in the one spare bedchamber and had already retired for the evening — Anthea and Rachel were making their way upstairs, with Rachel babbling on in praise of the evening's festivities.

'I heard no one complain,' Anthea stated.

'I am so excited. I think I shall not sleep at all tonight!'

'Are you?' Anthea eyed her curiously. 'It was a pleasant enough evening, but it scarcely merits a sleepless night.'

'Tell me, Thea,' Rachel asked earnestly, 'do you think that Quentin — Mr Safford — looks upon me as a woman, or merely as an amusing child?'

Anthea paused, her right foot on one step and her left on the step below.

'How do you look upon Mr Safford?' she tossed the question back at her.

'I—I do not know.' She sighed. 'There are times when he infuriates me, for he can be quite satirical. But most of the time I do enjoy his company immensely.'

'Well . . .' Anthea took her arm and they resumed their ascent. 'I like Mr Safford very much, and I think that he likes you more than he is willing to show.'

'Do you really?'

The eagerness in her voice was almost too comical, but Anthea knew better than to treat her feelings lightly. With all her common sense, Rachel was a girl of sensibility as well. Quentin Safford was her first love, to be sure, but she felt that this love would not be as ephemeral as most are. If Quentin played his cards right (and she knew him to be quite proficient at whist and speculation), Gideon might well find his daughter betrothed to be married before the end of the season.

'I do not want you to be breaking the young man's heart, Rachel.' She kept her voice level with some difficulty. 'He is too nice a gentleman to be trifling with.'

'As though I would do such a thing!' Rachel protested, unaware of any irony in the thought. 'But do you think that I *could* break his heart?'

'Quite easily, I should imagine.'

'I wonder if he could break mine?'

'As though he would do such a thing!' Anthea echoed her stepdaughter's own words, at which point they parted on the upper landing with a smile on both sides.

Altogether, it had been a most interesting evening, but she was glad to be finally joining her husband for the most enjoyable part of the night.

CHAPTER TWENTY: A CHANGE IN THE WIND

The next morning was a dismal-looking affair. Rain spattered on the windows, making everything outside look dull and indistinct. Anthea had promised Rachel and Sally to take them to Sydney Gardens for breakfast, but nobody cared to brave the elements. Instead, the ladies of the house slumped upon the drawing room sofa, feeling gloomy and abandoned after Gideon left to consult with one of his colleagues.

By early afternoon the skies had cleared and the two younger girls were much too restive to remain indoors. Besides, as Rachel reminded her, they were all supposed to purchase new gloves to wear tonight. Mr Safford had graciously invited the family and Rachel's young friend to accompany him to the theatre.

'I had completely forgotten our engagement with Quentin tonight,' Anthea confessed.

'How could you, Thea!' Rachel was aghast to think that something so momentous could have slipped her memory so easily.

Quentin was already so frequent a visitor to their home that Anthea had really grown quite inured to his presence among them. He had accompanied Rachel and Miss Quimby — always with one of their maids, of course — on walks around the city, and even ventured as far as Claverton Down on one occasion. He was obviously more than smitten with Rachel, and Anthea was inclined to think their eventual union almost inevitable. She felt that it would be beneficial to both, socially and privately as well.

* * *

As she dressed for the theatre some hours later, Anthea reflected that she had not seen her husband all day. She examined her gown of lilac crepe in the glass and liked its simplicity. She needed jewellery of some kind to set it off, however.

As this thought occurred to her, Gideon entered the room, bearing several small boxes, which he placed upon the dresser near the spot where she was standing. Judging from the size and shape of the boxes, they could only contain jewels. Did he know her so well that he was now able to read her thoughts?

'I have a gift for you, dearest,' he told her, coming up behind her and kissing the back of her neck in a way that made her shiver, though certainly not from cold.

'What is it?' she asked, reaching for the first box.

'You shall see,' he whispered mysteriously.

As she opened the first box, she gave a gasp. It was a set of garnet jewels *en parure*. There was a necklace, earrings and matching bracelets. It was not the quality or worth of the set, however, which made her catch her breath. She knew these jewels well, though it had been years since she had seen them.

'Mama's jewels!' she exclaimed, the tears gushing from her eyes. The smaller boxes contained an amber cross on a gold chain, a string of pearls with a coral pendant, and an ornate ring. 'How . . . how did you come by them, Gideon?'

He gave a slight cough before speaking.

'I've had them for years, Anthea.' He came up behind her once more, placing his hands upon her shoulders and resting his cheek against hers. 'When your father sold them to me, I knew that they must have belonged to your mother and would have meant so much more to you than even the most expensive of gems.'

'And you kept them.' She turned about, looking into his beautiful dark eyes and basking in the love she saw there. She knew now that he had kept that love hidden from their very first meeting. Looking into her own heart, she realized that she had also felt that instant bond, that something which was more than mere liking, but she had never dared even to admit it to herself.

'I always intended to give them to you as a wedding present,' he confessed, adding, 'I did not then know that I would be the very fortunate groom. I was waiting only for the right time, and tonight seemed appropriate.'

'If only I had something to give to you!' she cried, almost overwhelmed at his generosity.

He fished in his pocket, drawing out something which fit neatly into the palm of his hand.

'Here is something,' he said, smiling, 'which has already become my most highly prized possession.'

He held out his hand to display Mr Jagger's completed miniature. Looking down at the painted image of herself, Anthea was surprised at how young the girl staring up at her appeared.

'She looks happy, does she not?' Gideon asked.

'I never thought I should look that way again.'

'Sweetheart!' he murmured, drawing her against him in comfort rather than passion. 'If only I could erase all memories of sadness from your mind, my Anthea. If I could but help you to forget the years which were stolen from you.'

'Do not wish it, Gideon.' She sighed deeply and leaned against him. 'The woman you married is not the same girl who locked herself away from the world seven years ago. And it is better so.'

'Dearest?' He was surprised by this statement. To his prejudiced eyes, she was and always had been perfect.

'Before,' she told him, 'I was a giddy and silly girl with no thought for anything that was not frivolous or foolish.'

'But you were so young, my dear.' He was eager to exonerate her. 'Youth was made to be flighty and foolish, surely?'

'Perhaps,' she acknowledged. 'But that young and foolish girl could never have been worthy of such a man as you. You would not have looked twice at her.'

'Anthea!' He was almost angry now. 'Never talk such nonsense to me again.'

She smiled up at him, stroking his face with the tips of her fingers. How could she ever make him understand? He might not be willing to admit that he was her superior, but she knew it to be true.

'When I closed the door and shut the world out, I realized how meaningless my world had always been.' She kissed his cheek, the corner of her lips just brushing the edge of his. 'I was forced into reflection, and from that reflection came a knowledge I had never cared to cultivate before. I saw the truth about myself, about my friends, and about the pitiful thing I once called my life. Humility is a great teacher, Gideon. Before that, I would have been incapable of truly appreciating a man like you. Looking back, I see that those lost years were preparing me for a new life with the most wonderful man in the whole world.'

She kissed his cheek again, but this time he slowly turned his head to capture her lips with his.

'I love you, Anthea,' he whispered huskily. 'My dearest wife, I love you.'

'And I adore you,' she answered.

'Do you know, last night was the first time that you told me so?'

'Forgive me, my love. I assumed that you knew how I felt.'

'I certainly hoped that you felt the same way that I do.'

'But it is very good to hear it spoken, is it not?'

'Indeed it is.'

'Later tonight,' she promised against his mouth, 'I will tell you again . . . and show you as well!'

'I am quite sure that it will be by far the most satisfying part of the evening.'

* * *

Going down together, they found the girls in high spirits, laughing and chattering as they piled into Quentin Safford's carriage, hired specially for the occasion. The Guzmans had committed themselves to another engagement and were not accompanying them, but John and Lydia Savidge would be meeting them at the theatre.

The Theatre Royal was crowded. After all, *The School for Scandal* was a popular play — one of Mr Sheridan's finest. There was hardly an empty seat, for it seemed all the world had come to be entertained tonight. It was a well-designed, elaborately decorated building, with good lighting that enabled amorous gentlemen to spy their latest lady love in her box across the room. Their own box was a good one, giving them a fine view of the stage and close enough that they could easily hear the actors speaking their lines.

John and Lydia met them just as they were about to take their seats, and while they all settled in amid the usual murmurs and pointless conversation, Anthea's gaze travelled to the other side of the room. The box directly across from them was already occupied by a party of four, and even at this distance she could not fail to make out the features of two of them. Georgina was beautifully gowned, of course, and around her neck once again was the infamous necklace. Crispin looked wooden and uncomfortable, perhaps because he had observed Anthea looking at them.

Gideon noticed the direction of her gaze and squeezed her hand reassuringly. The play was about to begin, and everyone's attention was now directed toward the stage. Soon most of their party was absorbed in the antics going on beyond the footlights. But Lady Sneerwell and Mr Surface were no match for Mr and Mrs Flitwick. Anthea had to force herself to concentrate on the performance, though her mind could not be entirely fixed on what was going forward. Being conversant with the story, she managed to laugh and applaud in all the proper places, but she had never felt quite so uncomfortable and had never been so glad to see the play end.

CHAPTER TWENTY-ONE:
THE PLAY'S THE THING

As the patrons slowly made their way out of the theatre, Mr Safford's party found themselves suddenly directly beside Georgina and Crispin. Everyone bid a polite if distant 'good evening,' and that should have been the end of it. It was not.

'Excuse me, Mr and Mrs Savidge,' Georgina said imperiously, 'but my neighbour, Mr Tremblay, tells me that you have been asking a great deal of questions concerning my former maid, Nancy.'

'We have,' John replied briefly, in his usual rather indolent manner.

'I fail to see,' Mrs Flitwick snapped, 'what possible point there can be in meddling in other people's affairs.'

'And I fail to see, ma'am,' Lydia countered, not a whit discomposed, 'how our queries are any business of yours.'

'You are a most impertinent young woman,' Georgina almost spat the words at her, but Lydia remained unmoved.

'Strangely enough,' she said, 'you are not the first person to tell me so. Nor are you likely to be the last.'

'What are you about, I should like to know?'

'But I am not in the least inclined to tell you, and such high-handed treatment from a tradesman's daughter is unlikely to alter that inclination.'

Battle was now fairly joined, and the others merely watched with far more fascination than they had given to the play. Whether this might be comedy or drama, they were not sure, but it was undoubtedly entertaining. Georgina looked as if she would go off like a canon and was clearly unaccustomed to being treated thus. No toadeater was Mrs Savidge.

'We are here,' John put in smoothly, 'at the request of a friend, who wishes to discover the truth about the young woman's disappearance. We have already learned from Mr Tremblay that she definitely did not run off with the footman next door.'

'How can he be certain of that?' she demanded. 'Nancy was ever a fast piece, and that Chittering fellow was no better.'

'We have reason to suspect foul play,' Lydia added, giving the woman a direct look. Her gaze, meanwhile, briefly met her husband's. It was a moment of quiet satisfaction, for Georgina had just given them the name of the errant servant.

'Foul play!' Georgina repeated, almost stammering in her state of high dudgeon. 'I know not what you are implying, but if you continue in this vein, you will be very sorry, I assure you.'

'What are you afraid of?' Lydia was almost taunting the other woman now. 'The truth, perhaps?'

'I have never been so insulted in my life!'

'Have you not? You are undeservedly fortunate.' Her opponent remained maddeningly calm.

'Well, what can I expect,' Georgina shot back, 'from someone who is always in company with a Jew and a common thief!'

'One hardly knows which is worse,' Gideon said laconically at this point. 'A Jew or a thief.'

'I think that you should learn to bridle your wife's tongue,' she flung at John, apparently thinking she had tipped him a doubler.

'Your own husband,' he remarked, 'seems incapable of curbing your temper, ma'am. It must be a terrible trial to him.'

At this, Mrs Flitwick pulled her brocaded domino about her and made a most dramatic exit.

'She really should have been on the stage,' Rachel chuckled as the silent Crispin and his most voluble wife were once again lost in the crowd.

'But you,' Gideon said, smiling, 'were quite magnificent, Mrs Savidge. A formidable opponent indeed.'

* * *

As they walked out into the cool night air, everyone was preparing to return to their homes, but were unexpectedly forestalled by Gideon himself.

'I know the hour is late,' he said to John and Lydia, 'but if it is not too much trouble, I would greatly like to tell you something which might be pertinent to our quest.'

'We will be happy to accompany you there,' John was quick to acquiesce.

Miss Quimby was deposited at the door of her parents' house, quite befuddled by what she had just seen and heard. She was far more concerned about her gown, the hem of which had been torn slightly during their departure.

A very few minutes found them back at the Rodrigo residence, where they assembled in the front parlour. Gideon stepped out of the room for a few minutes, returning with a folded sheet of paper which he opened slowly while the others watched, mystified.

'This,' he said, holding the paper up to them, 'is a letter from Mr Solomon, a friend of mine in Bristol. He is a master in the manufacture of paste gems.'

The others perked up immediately at this statement.

'An astute move, Mr Rodrigo,' John said, nodding his approval.

'I wrote to Mr Solomon immediately after our encounter with the Flitwicks at the Upper Rooms. In my letter,

I described in some detail the necklace which Georgina Flitwick was wearing and asked if he knew of anyone in Bristol who might have made such a necklace at any time. His reply, delivered more speedily than I anticipated, by a friend who was coming to Bath, is most enlightening.'

'How exciting!' Rachel exclaimed. 'Do tell us what you learned, Papa.'

Her father smiled indulgently.

'As it happens, the paste necklace was made by none other than Mr Solomon himself.'

'Aha!' Lydia cried clapping her hands together and almost jumping out of her chair.

'It was commissioned by a good-looking young man . . .'

'What!' Anthea was surprised. 'Not by Georgina?'

'No indeed.'

'Do not tell me that it was Captain Flitwick himself who had it made!' This was from Lydia.

'No,' Gideon answered for the second time.

'Then who?'

'It was paid for by a Mr Chittering, some seven years ago.'

For once there was no outburst from the others. They were all quite speechless. At last John found his voice.

'Can it be that the footman and Georgina's maid had plotted and carried out so brazen a robbery?'

'I would imagine,' Quentin said, frowning, 'that such an excellent forgery would be reasonably costly as well. Would the two of these conspirators have had enough money for such a venture?'

'Unlikely, I should think,' was Gideon's assessment.

'It must be connected in some way,' John murmured, trying to puzzle it out.

'But how?' Lydia responded.

'It is certainly another interesting fact.' Anthea shrugged her shoulders. 'What it means, however, completely escapes me.'

'Chittering.' John repeated the one word, slowly enunciating every syllable. 'That name means something to me, but I cannot quite grasp the thread of it to see where it leads.'

'Perhaps a night's rest will help to clear the clutter in your head, sir,' Quentin said with a grin.

'You may well be right,' John agreed, rising from his chair.

'At any rate, a good night's sleep is clearly in order for us all,' Gideon decreed.

The party dispersed rapidly, Quentin repairing to his own lodgings while the Savidges walked along the well-lit street to their own temporary dwelling. Rachel bid her father and stepmother good night, and they made their way to their bedchamber. It is doubtful, however, that they got much sleep that night.

CHAPTER TWENTY-TWO:
AN UNEXPECTED ENCOUNTER

The following day was once again a dreary one, made more forlorn on Anthea's part by the arrival of yet another letter, this time summoning Gideon to London to attend to an important matter of business. He would be gone only for three or four days, but when he left the next morning, Anthea felt immediately and ridiculously bereft. Really, her attachment to him was growing quite excessive, she thought. After all, it was not as if he were going on an ocean voyage!

Even Rachel had deserted her today, spending the greater part of it with Sally and Mrs Quimby. To escape her own dismal thoughts and feelings, Anthea decided to call on Mrs Lynford. That lady was as kind as ever, though she expressed concern over the younger woman's rather wan appearance. She spent a pleasant hour with this old friend before walking the short distance home.

As she made her slow progression, Anthea suddenly felt that she could not bear to return to an empty house. True, Mrs Norton and the rest of the servants were there. But without Gideon the rooms would seem more like a prison. She needed fresh air, liberty and solitude. It was not so very far to Sydney Gardens, so she turned to the east rather than the west and soon found herself strolling through the grounds in the vain hope that the verdant setting might revive her flagging spirits, if only for an hour or two. But thoughts of Gideon followed her everywhere. She could not help but recall the night of the gala concert, when Rachel and Quentin had surprised her in Gideon's embrace. She walked through the very grotto, which did not seem at all enticing by daylight.

There were not many people about. A few hardy souls shared the grounds with her, but they were strangers who merely nodded and smiled in passing. She scarcely noticed them, lost in her own melancholy thoughts. So inattentive was she that it was some time before she became aware that the sky was darkening and a persistent breeze whispered that a light rain might be forthcoming.

She was suddenly startled by the sound of her name being called out.

'Anthea!'

Turning about, she was even more surprised to discover who was accosting her. Advancing towards her along the garden path was none other than Crispin Flitwick. His strides were quick and purposeful, and he was actually a little breathless when he caught up with her.

'I did not expect to see you here, Crispin.' She might have added that she was not pleased either.

'No.' His face suffused with colour, like a naughty child caught by a stern nursemaid. 'I followed you from Laura Place.'

'Followed me!' She had been too preoccupied to notice.

'I saw you as you left one of the houses there. I was across the street at some distance, but I recognized you at once.'

'Did you?'

'I have wanted to speak with you alone ever since we met at the Upper Rooms.'

'Did you?' She was aware that she was repeating herself but did not know what else to say to him. She was really very annoyed at having been interrupted when she wished to be alone.

'You are even more beautiful than I remembered, Anthea!' he said in a rush.

'Am I?'

'I have never forgotten you.' To her consternation, he reached out and caught her right hand in his. 'I have always loved you, Anthea. Always. When I saw you at the theatre the other evening, it was as though the years fell away — as if I had never been away from you.'

She snatched her hand away and stepped back a pace, looking him directly in the eyes.

'What nonsense is this, Crispin?' she demanded, unimpressed.

'Have you forgotten that you loved me once?' he asked, like some hero in an overwrought German drama.

'I do not know that I ever did.'

'What do you mean?' He was clearly startled by her cold reception of his declaration. 'Of course we loved each other.'

'I take leave to doubt that you ever loved anyone but yourself.' She almost smiled at his look of utter astonishment. 'As for me, I was a very young and silly girl who was ready to fall in love with the first handsome sprig who offered for me.'

He was absolutely aghast at this unromantic depiction of their previous connection.

'How can you dismiss what we felt so easily?'

'I know now what real love is,' she said simply. 'And what I felt for you was no more than a young girl's midsummer madness.'

'Do you mean to say,' he retorted, 'that you are actually in love with this — this Jew?'

'My husband,' she said, already weary of his common mind and threadbare emotions, 'is a better Christian than you can boast of being. And yes, I am quite hopelessly in love with him.'

His face grew darker than the gathering thunderclouds above them.

'I might have guessed as much,' he muttered ungraciously. 'After all, it is common report that nothing would do for you but to elope with him at dead of night. I would not have expected that sort of behaviour from you!'

'You do not know me very well, sir. And if you had truly loved me seven years ago, you would not have been so quick to jump to the conclusion that I was guilty, nor so eager for me to deliver your *congé*. You certainly turned to Georgina for solace with amazing alacrity.'

'I have little enough solace in my marriage, I can assure you,' he said bitterly.

'No doubt you have as much as you deserve.'

'I did not think you would be so cold-hearted, Anthea.'

He looked much aggrieved, which she found rather amusing. What, she wondered, had he expected? Did he presume that she would have consented to some sort of clandestine liaison with him? Was he bored? Was he curious? Perhaps he knew that her husband was away and assumed that she would not be averse to a little discrete dalliance in his absence. If so, he could not have been more mistaken. He had apparently taken her for Lady Teazle. Whatever the truth might be, it was no great matter. He was a part of her past, and she was more than content for him to remain so.

'Go back to your wife, Crispin,' she told him, not unkindly but without a shred of regret. 'If you do not love her, you had best learn how to do so.'

He laughed, but the sound was the reverse of happy. 'If you think she is a dutiful and angelic wife, Anthea, let me disabuse you of that illusion!'

'Whatever she may be is no concern of mine, thank God.'

'She is a monster,' he said, and for a moment Anthea thought she saw real fear in his eyes.

'What do you mean?' she demanded.

'There is nothing that she is not capable of.' He closed his eyes for a moment and drew a deep breath before continuing. 'If you knew what she really is, you would . . . well, never mind. But I suggest that you warn your two friends not to continue with their inquiries into Nancy's disappearance. Let the matter go, I beg of you.'

'Or what may happen?' she asked, feeling a surge of resentment that he should make such an absurd request.

'With Georgina, one never knows.' Crispin stared unseeingly at a bed of colourful flowers beside the path. 'I suspect that she knew more about that affair than anyone might guess. I have even thought that her own father's death might not have been a natural one, and that she . . . well, no matter.'

'In that case,' she answered, shocked and repelled by his suggestion, 'it is more imperative than ever for my friends to discover the truth of the matter.'

'On your head be it, then,' he said somewhat ominously. With more tenderness, he added, 'Well, she is the mother of my son. Were it not for him, I should have repudiated her long ago.'

What a charming family the Flitwicks seemed to be! Anthea wondered whether she was the only one who had been locked in a kind of prison for seven years. It seemed that Crispin had endured something equally galling. Perhaps she should not judge him so harshly, but she did wish that he would go away.

'I think you have said more than enough, sir,' she said, trying not to sound too much as if she were dismissing him — though she was.

'I will take my leave of you, then,' he said woodenly. 'I wish you every happiness, Anthea.'

'I shall be happy,' she replied, 'when my husband returns.'

'I wonder if he knows how very fortunate he is to be married to you.'

'Believe me, Crispin, I consider myself to be by far the most fortunate one in my marriage.'

* * *

Anthea returned home in a pensive mood, having been given much unsavoury meat to chew upon. Could Crispin have been telling the truth? Was his wife a monster? In what way?

It was several hours before Rachel came upstairs after her visit with the Quimby family. John and Lydia were invited for dinner, along with Quentin, and Anthea was glad of the company and the temporary distraction it provided. She hoped that by the time she retired for the evening, she might fall asleep at once from sheer tiredness. It was amazing how quickly she had gone from sleeping alone to a state in which it was almost impossible for her to sleep without her husband beside her.

Her guests arrived promptly at the appointed hour, and dinner was a subdued success. It was some time before they settled into their respective seats and dispensed with the mandatory pleasantries. At last it was Lydia who reintroduced the topic of Mrs Flitwick and the necklace.

'I think the woman must be touched in the upper works or something,' she announced, employing decidedly vulgar parlance.

'Her words could be construed as a vicious threat,' Lydia's husband agreed, though not a whit perturbed.

'I had the misfortune to run into Crispin this afternoon,' Anthea told them, and the others leaned forward in their eagerness to catch whatever scandalous tale she might be about to relate.

She recounted the events which unfolded in Sydney Gardens and had seldom spoken to a more receptive audience.

'So Georgina is a monster out of Mary Shelley's novel?' Rachel asked when she had finished her brief narration.

'She would not, perhaps, balk even at murder?' Lydia suggested.

Anthea shook her head. 'I can only say that he seemed to be genuinely afraid of her.'

'A big, strong, healthy and regimental young man!'

'A woman,' Lydia said with authority, 'can be every bit as cunning and cruel as any man. Believe me, we know.'

Everyone now focused on Lydia. It seemed that this young woman and her husband were well acquainted with evil in both male and female forms.

'But we are still in the dark,' Quentin contributed, 'concerning how, when and where the crime was committed.'

'And what part, if any, did Mrs. Flitwick play?'

'We seem to be at a decided disadvantage,' Lydia said, momentarily discouraged.

'We can hardly advertise in the *Bath Chronicle*, can we?' Anthea asked. '*Murderer sought for an undetermined crime which may or may not have been committed*!'

Spoken in jest, Anthea was completely unprepared for the reaction from John. He leapt to his feet, clapping his left hand against his forehead and crying out:

'Great God! Of course, that is it.'

'What on earth has got into you, John?' Lydia demanded, as mystified as the rest of them.

'Now I know,' he answered her, 'where I recalled the name of Chittering!'

'Well, where was it?'

'The *Sussex Advertiser*!' he said, then turned to Quentin and shot a question at him: 'What is the swiftest way to get from Bath to Pevensey in Sussex?'

'One might go by the Royal Mail coach,' Mr Safford replied.

'I must be off at once. I have not a moment to lose!'

They all continued to gape at him, wondering if he had taken leave of his senses.

'Where are you going, Mr Savidge?' Anthea asked.

'To Sussex, obviously,' Lydia said. 'But I still do not understand why.'

'There's no time to explain,' John said in a rush, and would have bolted out the door if Quentin had not detained him.

'But stay, sir!' the other man said insistently. 'Can you drive a high perch phaeton?'

'Yes indeed,' John assured him, halting his mad dash. 'Have you such a vehicle?'

'I do,' Quentin admitted, rising swiftly and going over to him. 'And there are several coaching inns where we can change horses.'

'We?' John asked, with a fleeting smile.

'I do not know where you are going, or why,' Mr Safford said with decision, 'but I'm damned if I'll let you keep this adventure all to yourself, sir!'

'Very well,' John acquiesced, since he could see that the other gentleman was determined. 'I only pray that we are not too late.'

'Too late for what?' his longsuffering wife asked.

'For the hanging!' he shouted back, already halfway through the door.

'Is an innocent man about to be hanged?' she demanded, more confused than ever.

'No, my dear,' he answered over his shoulder. 'A very guilty man indeed!'

CHAPTER TWENTY-THREE:
TWO MADWOMEN AND A CUP OF TEA

The three women were left in a state of bewilderment and disappointment that they should be cut out of what was clearly going to be a most entertaining romp. They commiserated with each other for some minutes, then turned to a discussion on the incomprehensible ways of the modern male. As it was quite late in the evening, Lydia bid them goodnight and made her way home. Anthea and Rachel each sought their own bed, and both of them fell almost immediately into a deep slumber, quite knocked about by the unprecedented events of the day.

They awakened late the following morning, and neither was in the best of moods. Anthea felt the absence of Gideon more acutely than ever, and Rachel grumbled about Quentin running off with Mr Savidge — which she considered totally unnecessary. They made a pathetic pair at breakfast, and then the arrival of Miss Quimby, accompanied by her maid, took Rachel out of the house before she could continue to add her might to her stepmother's gloom.

Soon after this, Lydia called on Anthea, and they attempted a more rational discussion of the events the previous evening. Lydia had searched in vain for the *Sussex Advertiser* her husband had mentioned, since that seemed to hold the key to his bizarre behaviour. As it turned out, however, most of it had been used by one of the maids to kindle the fire in the fireplace, and what remained proved useless.

After regaling her hostess with this piece of news, the two of them were interrupted by Mrs Norton, who brought in a note which had just been delivered to their door.

'Whatever can this be?' Anthea wondered aloud.

She broke the seal and read the few terse lines scribbled upon the paper, then looked up at Lydia, her eyes wide and staring in surprise.

'What is it, Anthea?'

'A note from Georgina.' She leaned forward, handing the paper over for her young friend to peruse.

'She apologizes for her behaviour at the theatre.' Lydia's brows rose. 'And she *requests* that you visit her for tea this afternoon.'

'What should I do?' Anthea was uncertain whether she wanted to see her former friend again.

'Based on her threats and the testimony of her husband,' Lydia said slowly, 'I do not think it would be wise for you to go alone.'

'But her invitation is not extended to anyone else,' Anthea protested. 'It would be very bad manners to bring someone along with me.'

'I will go with you,' Lydia said promptly.

'You?' Anthea actually laughed. 'She clearly detests you and poor John and is highly suspicious of your motives in asking so many questions of her neighbour. She would very likely throw the pair of us out of the house.'

'Oh, you need not worry.' Lydia smiled in her turn. 'She will not know that I am there.'

'Are you a magician, then?' her friend asked. 'Is invisibility among your other accomplishments?'

'Perhaps.' Lydia playfully tapped the tip of her own nose. 'I have my methods, however unorthodox they may seem.'

* * *

And so the afternoon found them wending their way to the Flitwick residence. It was not a very long walk, and they arrived without being either breathless or in a 'muck sweat', as Bunyan put it. Both were fashionably but demurely dressed, although Anthea noted Lydia's oversized and somewhat cumbersome reticule. They knocked at the door, which was shortly opened by a housemaid, who looked a little askance at being confronted by not one but two young ladies.

'Mrs Flitwick is expecting me,' Anthea said quickly.

'She is not expecting me,' Lydia added equally quickly, addressing the maid in a conspiratorial whisper. 'Now, listen to me, my girl. Here is a guinea for your trouble.'

'Certainly, ma'am.' The girl pocketed the coin and cocked her head to hear what role she was expected to play.

'I am going to take a brisk walk halfway down the street but will return in a trice. Be on the watch, for I will not knock.'

'Yes, ma'am.' She nodded happily. She had been well paid for what seemed a moment's work.

'You will let me in, and I shall be as silent as a spider while I keep watch outside the door to the room in which your mistress is entertaining this lady. Is that clear?'

'Yes, ma'am,' the girl repeated.

'Oh,' Lydia added, 'can you tell me who will be bringing in the tea tray?'

'That would be Fanny, ma'am.'

Lydia fished in her reticule and brought out another coin.

'Give this to Fanny,' she said, 'and tell her to take no notice of my presence outside the door and to say nothing to your mistress. If you should have any trouble from Mrs Flitwick later, you can find me at this address.' She handed her a small, folded piece of paper.

'Very well.'

Lydia flitted lightly down the street while Anthea braved herself to enter the lion's den. She was shown into a small sitting room, elaborately furnished in green and gold. Too ornamental and ostentatious for her own taste, it was a perfect foil for Georgina, who came toward her with arms outstretched as if she would clasp her to her plump bosom. She did not go that far but took Anthea's hands in her own and burst into speech.

'My dear Anthea, how long it has been!' For all the world, her visitor thought, as if they had both been circumnavigating the globe these seven years and had missed each other in passing.

'That is not my fault, Georgina,' Anthea answered, which brought the colour briefly into the other woman's cheeks.

'It is time for us to forget the past,' she declared, 'and bind up old wounds in true and honest friendship.'

Why, Anthea wondered, did she always have to sound like a character in a tawdry Restoration drama?

'Do sit down while I ring for tea.'

They both seated themselves and Georgina picked up a small bronze bell which she rang vigorously. Like her, it was surprisingly loud for its size.

Moments later another maid brought in the tray with sweetmeats and the usual accoutrements. She placed it on the small table between the two ladies, curtsied and withdrew immediately. As she did so, Anthea glanced toward the open doorway and saw Lydia peeping around it. She had a perfect view of the two ladies within, who were seated at an angle so that Georgina could not perceive her, but she was able to see them both, as well as the tea table.

'I shall pour,' Georgina began. She dispensed the tea into two delicate porcelain cups, added sugar as requested, and then took up a spoon to stir. As she lifted it, however, it fell from her hand onto the floor with a clatter and landed at Anthea's feet. Automatically, Anthea bent to retrieve it, straightening up after a brief moment.

'How clumsy I am!' Georgina exclaimed, with a conscious smile.

'It is no great matter. There is another spoon which will do as well.'

'So there is.' She was all smiles now, stirring briskly before handing her friend her cup. Anthea raised it to her lips.

'I would not do that if I were you, my dear Anthea.'

It was not Georgina who spoke these words. As Anthea lowered the cup, Lydia stepped into the room, her face hard and a decidedly belligerent look in her eyes.

'You!' Georgina snapped, staring at her with concentrated hatred. 'How did you get in here?'

'That is scarcely to the point, is it?' Lydia countered. 'The fact is that I am here now, and I would like to know what you poured into Mrs Rodrigo's cup when she bent to retrieve the spoon.'

'I?' Georgina looked a little flustered. 'I did no such thing.'

'But you did,' Lydia corrected. 'I saw you.'

'How could I possibly have done such a thing so quickly?' her opponent demanded.

'Obviously you have had some practice before.' Lydia folded her arms and gave her look for look. 'There is a small compartment in that large and rather gaudy ring you are wearing. It took only a moment to open it, deposit the powder within into Anthea's tea, and address her as if nothing had happened.'

'You are quick to accuse me, madam,' Georgina said, a self-satisfied look on her face. 'But you have absolutely no proof.'

'Well, then,' Lydia said, perfectly calm, 'since neither of you has yet taken a sip of tea, you will not mind switching cups and drinking the tea which you offered to your guest.'

'I will do no such thing!' Georgina stood up, looking from one woman to the other, finally directing her grievances at Anthea. 'You should really beware of the company you keep, Mrs Rodrigo. I invited you here today in the spirit of true friendship, and this is the thanks I receive.'

'With such friends as you are,' Lydia replied, 'Anthea has no need of enemies.'

'It certainly should be no hardship to drink my tea instead of yours,' Anthea added, placing her cup back onto the tray. 'Unless there is something amiss with mine?'

'I'll show you what I think of your attempts to slander my name!' the other woman cried, catching hold of the edge of the small table and tipping it over so that the table crashed to the floor, scattering the contents and breaking most of the tea service. 'Now neither of us can drink anything at all!'

She seemed hugely pleased with herself, and Anthea sat staring at her, wondering how she had ever considered this woman her friend. Her mask of good breeding was stripped away to reveal the unpleasant truth behind it.

'You have quite a vicious and unbridled temper, Georgina,' she said, surveying the mess at her feet and the face of her hostess. 'I think I never knew you until today.'

'And you are a plaster saint, I suppose,' Georgina flung at her. 'Did you think I was unaware of your clandestine meeting with my husband in Sydney Gardens yesterday? Did you?'

'Our meeting was quite accidental, and hardly clandestine, since we were in full view of anyone who passed by — which is how you learned of it, I presume.'

'You lie!' She was almost screeching now, and the maid who had answered the door appeared, having heard the commotion. This prompted Georgina to momentarily direct her wrath at the unfortunate servant. 'Be off with you before I send you packing!'

She wasted no time in doing what her mistress asked, and the lady turned once more on Anthea.

'My dear Georgina,' Anthea rose and looked at her with a combination of pity and disgust, 'I assure you that I have no designs on Crispin.'

'You have always wanted him,' she contradicted, glaring. 'But if you think that I will let you take him from me, you are very wide of the mark.'

'I have my own husband,' Anthea assured her, 'whom I find infinitely more desirable than yours.'

'A filthy Jew?' Georgina sneered, and Anthea, losing her temper at last, slapped her across the face.

'Never refer to my husband in such language again!' she said through clenched teeth, while Georgina put a hand up to her cheek.

This was too much for the other woman, who all but flung herself at Anthea, reaching out to grab her by the throat. She was smaller, but amazingly strong, and might well have overpowered the taller lady. Neither of them, however, had noticed Lydia reach into her rather large reticule and extract an elegant muff pistol. She stepped forward and placed the end of the barrel against Mrs Flitwick's temple before that lady could even press her fingers into Anthea's smooth, pale flesh.

'Are you mad?' Georgina cried, releasing Anthea and stepping back at once, looking at the gun in Lydia's hand.

'If I am, then we are evenly matched,' she answered, her voice as cool as an autumn breeze and her hand perfectly steady as she pointed the weapon at the other woman, 'Would you like me to demonstrate just how mad I am?'

'Get out.' Georgina spat the words at both of her visitors. Clearly she had expected no opposition to whatever scheme she had concocted for the woman she saw as a threat to her marriage.

'With pleasure,' Lydia said before directing her attention to Anthea. 'Shall we go, Mrs Rodrigo?'

'Certainly.' Anthea turned to accompany her young friend, then looked back at Georgina and added, 'Thank you for a most — stimulating — visit. Good day.'

Mrs Flitwick's bosom was heaving as she watched them leave, a look of sheer malignity on her face.

* * *

Lydia and Anthea were eager to exit the residence and made their way slowly back to the Rodrigo house. As they walked, there was only one topic which occupied their minds.

'I knew that she was plotting something,' Lydia said, shaking her head.

'I would like to know what it was that she put in my tea!'

'It might have been some kind of sedative, but I am inclined to believe that it was something worse.'

'But why?' Anthea was incredulous.

'Clearly,' Lydia replied, 'the woman is unhinged. She is quite diabolical, and I do not doubt that she would have dispatched you if she could have.'

'She appears to have a fixation on Crispin. Why she should think that I would still want him is beyond me.'

They looked left and right before crossing over to the other side of the street, and Lydia could not resist resorting to her own theory.

'She may well have killed before in order to ensure that you did not marry him.'

'I can well believe it after today's performance.' Anthea gave a little shudder. 'I am very glad that you insisted on accompanying me.'

'It has been a most instructive afternoon.'

'But why, in Heaven's name, do you carry a pistol in your reticule?' Anthea could not refrain from asking. 'Do you always have it about you?'

'No.' Lydia shook her head, then provided a brief explanation. 'John gave it to me and instructed me how to fire it properly. Considering the incidents in which we have taken part, one never knows when it might be of use. I had a premonition that I would have need of it today.'

'I wish that Gideon were here.' Anthea sighed.

'I am sure that he will not remain in London any longer than is strictly necessary.' She chuckled, adding, 'I daresay he is quite as eager to get back to you as you are for his return.'

'Are we very tiresome?' She could not resist a smile.

'Not as much as one might imagine.'

'Do you not wish for John's swift return?'

'Very much so,' Lydia answered, then spoilt any romantic notions which her friend might harbour by saying, 'I am going quite mad trying to decipher what his parting words might mean and wondering what he and Mr Safford are up to!'

'Do you think he will stop a man from hanging?'

'If anyone can do so, it will be John.' Her confidence in her husband was more reassuring than Anthea wished to admit.

'More importantly, will it have any bearing on my own dilemma?'

'From his extraordinary haste, I would say that it is most assuredly the key to everything we have been trying to establish about the jewels and the disappearance of the maid, Nancy.'

They both agreed to say nothing to Rachel about the events of the afternoon. Lydia told her friend to warn her servants to be especially vigilant, that no suspicious person lurking about the house should gain access to them.

'Good God!' Anthea exclaimed. 'I had not thought that Georgina would try something else after today's exhibition.'

'I must say that I think her husband quite right in his opinion that she is capable of almost anything.'

CHAPTER TWENTY-FOUR:
THE WANDERERS RETURN

The following afternoon brought an answer to Anthea's most fervent prayer: Gideon returned with little fanfare, but with an ardour which demanded immediate satisfaction. They spent a pleasant hour together in his bedchamber, and then Anthea acquainted him with the stirring events of the past three days. To say that he was angered at what had occurred in the Flitwick house was an understatement. She believed that, had he been near enough, he would have treated Georgina to the same treatment she had intended for his wife, and throttled her!

'Well,' Anthea said, attempting to pacify him, 'thanks to Lydia, I am alive and quite well.'

'I am more certain than ever that it was the right thing for me to do, to bring them to Bath.'

'They are a courageous pair, to be sure!' Anthea could not help a laugh escaping her. 'I was never more surprised than when I saw her extract that pistol from her reticule. But by her speech and manner, we might have been discussing the latest fashions from London.'

'For a couple so young, they are quite remarkable.' He hugged her closer, kissing her forehead. 'I do believe that they will solve this mystery and restore your good name, my love.'

'I hardly dare hope for such an outcome.'

'Then I will hope for us both.'

He frowned slightly, before reverting to a previous incident.

'Your encounter with Crispin?' he asked, a little hesitantly. 'I know what he has meant to you in the past.'

There was a delightful little pout to his lips, and she knew that her answer to this question was more important to him than he wished to show.

'He meant a great deal to the green girl I was then,' she admitted. 'But I am a woman now and find that my desires are much different.'

'He is a veritable Adonis,' he suggested. 'Far more handsome than I am.'

'Not in my eyes,' she stated.

'But he was your first love.' He scowled a little as he said this.

'Yes, he was my first love.' She brushed a stray lock of hair from his forehead. 'And if everyone were to marry their first love, what a sorry world this would be!'

'No regrets?' he queried.

'Not even one.'

'He kissed you first.'

'You kissed me best.'

'You intended to marry him.'

'But instead of marrying my first love,' she whispered against his lips, 'I married my true love. And I would so much rather be with my true love: my Gideon.'

After this, there was a considerable period when there was no talk at all. When they finally resumed their discussion, they were both satisfied that they were exactly where they wanted to be and with whom.

'My only regret,' Anthea confessed at last, 'is that we wasted five years being proper and circumspect, when you could at least have made a push to ask me to be your mistress.'

'No man of honour would behave in such a manner,' he protested. 'You were my love, not my lightskirt.'

'You did not wish to kiss me?' she demanded. 'You did not want to make love to me?'

'I wished to do everything we have done since our marriage,' he admitted, holding her closer. 'But I could hardly take such advantage of you and still consider myself a gentleman.'

'You might at least have tried to — to have your way with me!'

He was surprised at her attitude. She was almost angry with him, not for desiring her but for refraining from any attempt to seduce her!

'You would have been horrified — and rightly so — if I had done such a thing.'

'You impute to me far more virtue than I possess,' she argued. 'When a woman is in love, she wants a man's passion, not his honour. After all, you must know that I was lusting after you as well.'

'I am sure you never did such a thing,' he contradicted.

'Oh, I did not know it myself.' She smiled suddenly. 'I was far too ignorant to be aware of what my feelings for you truly were, and hardly dared to believe it myself. But I did think you very handsome, and I made sure to be below stairs whenever you visited Papa, that I might at least catch a glimpse of you.'

'Did you, sweetheart?' he murmured against her neck.

'My heart has been telling me forever that it belonged to you.' She wrapped her arms about his neck. 'Now, at last, I can say what before I could only feel.'

* * *

The next day, Gideon was closeted in his study, dealing with business which had not been attended to in his short absence. Rachel, after a happy reunion with him the previous evening, was eager to get out of the house.

'It is a fine day,' she told her stepmother, 'and a walk would be just the thing for such a morning.'

This recalled Anthea to her sense of duty regarding Rachel's coming out into society. She would not fob everything off onto her abigail. Apart from feeling a trifle guilty for neglecting her role, she knew that Gideon would be busy for most of the day and there was no point in being at home without his company.

It was indeed a lovely English morning, and the entire populace seemed to have the same idea as the two young ladies. They encountered a number of acquaintances who slowed their progress considerably. There were the invariable cuts and malicious whispers from high sticklers who still refused to countenance any dealings with someone reputed to be a thief. But Anthea was growing used to this, and Rachel simply stuck her tongue out at them behind their retreating backs.

Arriving at the Pump Room (always a place to meet acquaintances old and new), Rachel soon spied Miss Quimby and deserted Anthea in order to hear the latest news from her friend. She had hardly moved before she returned with Sally and nudged her uncomfortably in her side.

'There is a gentleman across the room who has been looking at you intently these five minutes or more,' Rachel whispered. 'I think he is about to approach you.'

Anthea immediately assumed that it was Crispin and was angry to think that he would inflict his attentions on her a second time. When she turned her head, however, she found herself confronting her father. It was their first meeting since the evening she had quit his house, and she was astonished at how well he looked. Indeed, she had not seen him so sober and so neatly dressed in years.

'Papa! I did not expect to see you here,' she exclaimed involuntarily.

'Good morning, Anthea.' His voice was steady, his demeanour unexpectedly conciliatory. 'May I introduce Mrs Marsden to you? Mrs Marsden, this is my daughter, Mrs Rodrigo.'

There followed a bewildering round of introductions between Sir Harry, Rachel, Miss Quimby and Mrs Marsden, in which so many names were exchanged as must surely be forgotten without further meetings in the future. Mrs Marsden, they learned, was the widow of a solicitor. She was an attractive but respectable-looking woman of the same age as Sir Harry. They had been introduced by a mutual friend, and quickly developed a rapport which boded well for a more intimate connection. If her father's improved appearance was this lady's doing, Anthea was more than happy to make her acquaintance.

Sir Harry drew her aside for a few moments and addressed her somewhat awkwardly but with what seemed real contrition.

'I know that I have not been the best of fathers to you, Anthea,' he said. 'Indeed, I blamed you for marrying Mr Rodrigo, but the truth is that it was my own shortcomings which led to a situation in which you had little choice but to accept any reasonable offer a gentleman might make to you.'

'You need not distress yourself on my account, Papa,' Anthea answered him. 'I am very much in love with Gideon and consider myself the most fortunate of women. I would not change my present place with anyone in the world.'

'I am glad, for your sake,' he said, his eyes not quite able to meet hers. 'Mr Rodrigo has been very generous to me, and I regret my behaviour toward him more than I can say.'

'I do not think that you will find him unforgiving, Papa.'

Sir Harry smiled. 'He will forgive me for my daughter's sake, no doubt.'

'He is more likely to forgive you because he has a forgiving nature,' she replied, smiling in her turn.

'You are not looking quite the thing, my dear,' he said suddenly.

'I have not been feeling well — at least in the mornings — for almost a fortnight now,' she admitted. 'But by the afternoon I am generally better.'

'I understand, child.' He nodded his head. 'Your mother was just the same. It will probably pass within another week or two.'

She looked at him, puzzled by his strange utterance. Then, quite suddenly, his meaning became clear and she felt her cheeks warming.

'Yes,' she stammered a little, 'I am sure you are right.'

'Your stepdaughter is an enchanting young lady,' he said. 'I look forward to meeting her again soon — and my son-in-law as well.'

'I will be happy to see you at any time.' She kissed him briefly on the cheek. 'And pray bring Mrs Marsden with you whenever you call upon us.'

'Thank you, my dear.' He sighed but seemed more cheerful. 'It is a courtesy I scarcely deserve.'

This was indeed a changed Sir Harry! She could hardly recall seeing him so affable and so eager to please. His attitude displayed his willingness to forget the past and to return to something like the closeness he had enjoyed with his daughter before the death of his wife. Anthea felt as if a heavy burden had been lifted from her. At least she need not fear an accidental meeting between them in the days to come.

* * *

Returning home, the Rodrigo ladies were startled to find none other than Mr Safford at their front door, preparing to enter. 'How wonderful to see you again!' Rachel exclaimed in an unguarded moment before collecting herself and adopting a more proper manner.

'It is always a pleasure, Miss Rodrigo,' Quentin said more formally, but lifted her hand and kissed it quite in the grand manner.

'Well, you had better come in,' Anthea said, and the three of them crossed the threshold together.

'But what about your business with Mr Savidge in Sussex?' Rachel asked, forestalling Anthea. 'Were you successful in preventing a hanging?'

'No indeed,' he replied. 'The gentleman in question should be swinging from the gallows this very afternoon.'

'You seem remarkably cheerful for one whose enterprise has failed,' Anthea remarked, feeling sadly crestfallen.

'But we did not fail.' He gave an impish grin. 'In fact, our efforts have been a resounding success.'

'In what way?' She was perfectly mystified.

'I think,' he answered, this time more grave, 'that we have solved the mystery of the maid's disappearance, and that your reputation will very shortly be restored, Mrs Rodrigo.'

'Is this true?'

It was Gideon who was speaking now, having heard voices in the hallway and emerged from his study.

'Good afternoon, Mr Rodrigo,' Quentin greeted him. 'Yes, we have accomplished what we set out to do — and not a moment too soon. Only one link in the chain of events must be unearthed in order to complete the true story of what happened seven years ago. This will be the final proof of your wife's innocence.'

'Are you sure of this?' Gideon Rodrigo demanded. 'You have proof?'

'As I say, the ultimate proof should be revealed this very day. In preparation for which, Mr Savidge has requested that we all gather here tomorrow morning, when he shall explain everything.'

'You are quite certain, then?'

'My dear sir,' Quentin said with an air of triumph, 'I urge you not to doubt this. I must admit that I thought John Savidge a candidate for Bedlam when we set out. But when I witnessed his masterful handling of so fantastic a situation, I could not but applaud his peculiar genius.'

'So we are to wait until tomorrow?' Gideon was not pleased with what seemed an unnecessary delay.

'We are certain of what the outcome will be,' Quentin assured him, 'but John wishes to have everything in order before he places the particulars before you.'

'Very well, then. It appears that we must wait on Master Savidge's discretion.'

CHAPTER TWENTY-FIVE: MURDER WILL OUT

Not surprisingly, none of the people involved in this unusual endeavour were able to rest easily in their beds that night. The next morning, Gideon was unusually solemn and Anthea felt as though her nerves were a harp on which a particularly inept musician was practicing. It was all most unsettling. Only Rachel was perfectly at ease. After all, if Quentin said that all was well, then all *must* be well. How could it possibly be otherwise?

Anthea forgave her for her partiality, and only wished she could be as sanguine about the situation. What could John be about to reveal which would reverse the course of the last seven years? It seemed all too fantastic to be true.

John and Lydia had also been awake most of the night. He had much to tell her, though she imagined that her own amazement was not as acute as that of the Rodrigos was likely to be, for much of what he explained to her was only what she had already correctly surmised. But it was with great antici-pation that the two of them made their way to the home of their patrons with news that would shake the foundations of Bath society but would surely be most welcome to their new friends.

It was almost noon before the small company gathered in the neat parlour of the Rodrigo house. All eyes were upon

John, whose figure, framed by the window, took on the stature of a prophet about to speak forth the word of the Lord to a trembling people. Nor was that impression entirely without justification.

'When my wife and I first read Mr Rodrigo's letter,' John began with slow deliberation, 'we hesitated to accept his flattering offer, for it seemed a near impossible task to discover what might have happened some seven years before. But neither of us is averse to a challenge, so we agreed to do all in our power to fulfil his commission.'

'After meeting the Rodrigo family,' Lydia continued, taking up the tale, 'we agreed that it was most unlikely that Mrs Rodrigo could be guilty of theft.'

'There seemed to be little mystery regarding the identity of the true culprit.' John looked about him, as if questioning whether anyone there might disagree, but no one spoke. 'Anthea's friend, Georgina Flitwick, was the only one who had access to the jewels in question, and a motive for committing such a heinous act. The difficulty lay in proving her involvement.'

'We quickly learned,' Lydia said, glancing up at him briefly for corroboration, 'that the key to the mystery of what had happened was the disappearance of the maid, Nancy — who, despite what everyone believed, had not eloped with the neighbour's footman.'

'I'm afraid,' John gave an apologetic grimace, 'that I have been an unpardonable slow-top.'

'In what way?' Rachel asked, taken aback by his unwonted humility.

'The moment that I heard the name *Chittering*,' he explained, 'I should have remembered where I had encountered it, but it was the next day before I could recall where I had heard or seen the name before.'

'It was Anthea herself,' Lydia nodded in her direction, 'whose chance remark about advertising for a criminal brought back to my husband the knowledge of where he had seen the name and in what connection.'

As it happened, John had brought with them from Sussex the key to the mystery. It had been with them all the time, in the *Sussex Advertiser*, without anyone being aware of its significance. In between stories of a mermaid and a missing child, was the news of a man charged with murdering his elderly employers. The man, of course, was Edwin Chittering himself.

'Do not tell me,' Anthea pleaded, 'that he killed poor Nancy as well.'

'I'm afraid that he did exactly that,' John contradicted her.

'Oh dear God!' she cried. 'Why would they murder the maid?'

'To answer that,' Lydia explained, 'we must go back to the original crime, which was never meant to include murder.'

'What then?' Gideon questioned intently.

'From the moment that Anthea accepted Crispin Flitwick's offer of marriage,' Lydia said, locking her fingers together in front of her as she concentrated on what she was about to say, 'Georgina was determined to discredit her in some way which would almost certainly end their betrothal. She wanted Crispin for herself. He was hers, and nobody else could be allowed to have him.'

'Remember,' John elaborated, 'that Anthea had already revealed to her friend that she had a secret hiding place for her own jewels, which were not nearly as valuable as those of Miss Shield.'

'Did Georgina visit you shortly before the theft of the necklace was discovered?' Lydia prompted Anthea.

'That morning, she came to the house with her maid — with Nancy — and, in the course of her visit, asked me to play a favourite song on the pianoforte.'

'Ah!' Lydia looked very pleased with herself. 'And where did Nancy go?'

'I . . . I do not know,' Anthea admitted, surprised that she had never considered this before.

'On the instructions of her mistress,' John informed her, 'she slipped upstairs, turned up the carpet, lifted the floorboard, and removed the necklace before anyone could catch her.'

'It was very daring!' Rachel exclaimed. 'She might have been seen at any time.'

'And she would have made some excuse that her mistress had sent her to fetch something from Miss Halliwell's bedchamber. But, in all honesty, she took many risks and it is amazing that she was so successful.'

'I suppose nobody would have been likely to doubt her,' Rachel conceded.

'And yet,' Lydia stated, rising from her seat to stand beside her husband, 'it was really the weakest link in the whole business.'

'How so?'

'Because,' Gideon answered before either of the Savidges could do so, 'she had to admit the maid into her confidence and make her a party to the conspiracy.'

'Exactly so.' John beamed his approval.

At first everything had gone just as she had planned. Everyone believed Anthea guilty of the crime, and Crispin was released from his betrothal — much to his own relief. Miss Shields soon realized, however, that by employing the maid in such a way — both to purloin the necklace and then to impersonate Anthea with the jeweller — she had made a serious mistake. Nancy soon started to make demands and issue veiled threats of informing the authorities what she had done. At first Georgina acquiesced and gave her extra pocket money and trinkets. But she very soon came to the conclusion that she would never be safe from detection as long as Nancy was alive.

'She had achieved her primary objective,' Lydia stated, with a nod to Anthea, 'which was to destroy her friend's reputation and ingratiate herself with Crispin.'

'It was truly despicable,' Rachel snapped, her cheeks pink with indignation at such casual cruelty.

'There could hardly be anything more so,' Anthea agreed. 'In the words of Shakespeare, *Who steals my purse, steals trash . . . But he who filches from me my good name, robs me of that which not enriches him and makes me poor indeed.'*

'But come,' Gideon drew them back to the subject at hand. 'What action did Miss Shields take, and how does it involve the Chittering fellow?'

Both Lydia and John paused in their narrative, and it was Quentin who took up the tale at this point.

'I must confess that I was as bewildered as anyone when John and I began our heroic dash into Sussex.' He shook his head and glanced at John, silently seeking his approval before continuing. As John nodded, Quentin said, 'Only when it was explained to me that the *Sussex Advertiser* which the Savidges brought with them from their home contained the story of a certain Edwin Chittering who had confessed to murdering his aged employers, did I see the connection. It was highly unlikely that two men with the same name could be involved in two separate crimes — especially as the Flitwicks' neighbour had been positive that the same man was now in Sussex, as he had seen and spoken with him.'

The problem was that it was highly probable that they would be too late to question the man, as he might already have been hanged for this second crime, without anyone being the wiser concerning his previous criminal activities.

'It happened that Mr Chittering's hanging had been delayed due to inclement weather and the consequent late arrival of Mr Mopsley, the Justice of the Peace, in Alfriston.'

'Still, we were most fortunate,' Quentin told them, 'that we had some influence in the matter, what with *my* father's rank and the fact that John's father was an old friend of Mr. Mopsley.'

'It seems,' Gideon noted with a slight chuckle, 'that fortune does indeed favour the bold.'

'Just so,' Quentin seconded this opinion.

Upon receiving permission to speak with the condemned man, they ventured into the local gaol to find a good-looking and well-groomed individual who was loquacious and seemed rather proud of his achievements in the line of murder. He was perfectly unrepentant and eager to tell his story in chilling and gruesome detail. The killing of his previous employers was of minor interest to the other two men, but they allowed him to expatiate on the callousness of the gentry, who showed no compassion upon a poor servant whose pilfering was, to his own mind, perfectly justifiable on the grounds that he had accrued a rather large gaming debt.

'Eventually,' John added, bringing things back to Bath some seven years before, 'he related the events which led to his absconding, leaving behind rumours of a clandestine liaison with the maid.'

In truth, Chittering never had many dealings with Nancy. He had made advances to her, which she spurned with a haughtiness quite out of keeping with her situation in life. It was, he told them, Georgina who was not averse to a kiss and a cuddle with a man who might be her social inferior but had a handsome face and an impudence which she found curiously exciting. When Crispin Flitwick appeared on the scene, however, their clandestine meetings came to an end. She 'set her cap at him', to use a common phrase, in the most outrageous way, but he had eyes only for her friend, Miss Halliwell. When Anthea accepted his offer of marriage, Miss Shields transformed into a raging virago, bent on revenge for having been deprived of what she considered her rightful property. She was an heiress, after all, and the darling of her doting papa. She must and should have anything she wanted — even the fiancé of another woman.

* * *

'And at last,' Lydia chimed in, 'we come to the fate of the hapless Nancy.'

Tired of Nancy's increasing demands and hints of exposure, Georgina simply decided to get rid of her as quickly and completely as possible. Not the cleverest of criminals, she administered a sedative draught to the girl in a glass of milk (enough to disable a horse, according to Mr Chittering) before her bedtime and waited for her to fall asleep.

'It was here,' John announced without any flourish, 'that she made her ultimate mistake, which cost her dearly.'

'What was that?' the three Rodrigos asked in unison.

'She was not quite up to killing the girl herself and disposing of the body. Her own small stature and her inexperience in such matters made it necessary for her to enlist the services of an accomplice.'

'Chittering.'

'Naturally.' Now it was Quentin's turn to once again narrate a portion of this convoluted tale.

Chittering's relation of the events which occurred that night was chilling enough and hearing it even at second-hand made the others shiver. The two of them bound and gagged the insensible girl and, carrying her down the back stairs, propped her up beside him in a small gig which he borrowed from his employer (without the employer's knowledge, needless to say). They drove to the edge of St James's cemetery, where he unloaded his bundle and placed it behind a convenient yew tree.

'What happened next,' Lydia spoke in a hushed voice, as if squeezing the words out through a parched throat, 'is something I do not care to think of.'

Chittering had removed a sharp knife from Mr Tremblay's kitchen. He stabbed the still-unconscious girl several times about the body. The effects of the sedative must have just begun to dissipate, however, and at the first thrust of the knife she sat up unexpectedly and stared at him a moment through sightless eyes. It had, he said, given him 'quite a turn', though not so much as to prevent him from finishing his gruesome task.

'He buried her in the cemetery?' Gideon asked.

'He did indeed,' Lydia answered.

'But surely,' Anthea commented faintly, sickened by such a horrific deed conducted with such brazen unconcern. 'Surely, even if no one saw him burying the body, a freshly dug grave would have been easily discovered and aroused suspicion.'

'Ah!' This was Quentin once more. 'That is where he showed some imagination.'

'How so?' Anthea wondered aloud.

'There had been a funeral there only that afternoon, and the soil from the freshly dug grave was still soft and loosened,' John explained, putting his arm about his wife as she flinched involuntarily. 'He was able to accomplish the interment more quickly and with far less effort.'

The murderer simply dug his way down to the coffin, deposited Nancy's body on top of it, and once more filled the hole with the same soil. He then returned to the gig and drove it back to Mr Tremblay's residence.

'But what if someone had seen him?' Rachel cried, as astonished as the rest.

'As he had every intention of disappearing that night,' Lydia commented, 'it would have been assumed that he was using the gig to run off with the maid!'

'Of course,' she said, adding, 'But you spoke of a price which Miss Shields had to pay for his assistance.'

'Miss Georgina intended to fob him off with a few pounds for his heroic labours,' John said. 'But Edwin Chittering was no Nancy to be fobbed off with trinkets and pocket money! Not he. He demanded something of far more value.'

'The necklace!' Gideon said at once.

'Yes.'

Chittering told the young woman that if she did not hand over to him the infamous jewels, he would expose her to the world. He agreed, however, to have a copy made by the best man in the business, who was in Bristol. Georgina dutifully supplied him with a letter for the jeweller explaining that she wanted something as close to the original as possible, as she did not wish to travel with such a priceless possession, which would be a magnet for every highwayman and footpad.

'I do not understand,' Rachel voiced a reservation concerning the business, 'why she did not simply say at the outset that Anthea had stolen the jewels and hidden them in her father's house?'

'In the first place,' Lydia pointed out, 'she would have had to prove that they had been stolen by Anthea — which she could only have done if she knew the hiding place. And the question might have arisen that if she knew all along where they might be, why she did not go and search for them herself.'

'Also,' John said, 'there would likely have been fewer people who would have believed her. She was not universally admired, with her airs and graces, and some would have doubted her story. But the addition of the veiled lady and the evidence of the jeweller seemed to give incontrovertible proof of Miss Halliwell's guilt.'

'So, what happens now?' Anthea asked.

'We have already given Mr Chittering's signed confession to the authorities.'

'And,' Quentin added, 'they have unearthed the remains of a young woman, whose body was buried atop the coffin of a Mr De'Ath — which piece of evidence Mr Chittering related with a pronounced laugh that quite chilled me to the bone.'

'It is all so fantastic, I can hardly believe it,' Anthea said. 'After all this time . . .'

'Now all of Bath will know what I have known all along,' Gideon planted a kiss on his wife's brow. 'Your innocence can never again be questioned.'

CHAPTER TWENTY-SIX: JUSTICE AND MERCY

The discovery of Nancy's corpse in the cemetery and the arrest of Mrs Flitwick was as sensational as any event in that sedate town had ever been. Never had the good citizens heard of anything so gruesome or so incredible. The saga of the top-lofty Mrs Leigh Perrot had now been eclipsed by the most fantastic revelations which would put even Mrs Radcliffe to shame.

John and Lydia decided to extend their visit to Bath. Having become fast friends with the Rodrigos, they wished to enjoy their company and to continue sampling the delights of the town before they returned to Sussex. They were now able to consider it in the nature of a holiday, without the strain of searching for the source of calumny and murder.

'I understand,' John said one afternoon, over tea, 'that Mrs Flitwick treated the gapers to quite a fit of histrionics as she was led away by the authorities.'

'The language she employed,' Mrs Lynford said, as one who had been a witness to the entire episode, 'was such as no woman can use and still call herself a lady.'

'It appears,' Lydia added, 'that she blamed all of her misfortunes on poor Anthea.'

'That is no great thing.' John was philosophical about it. 'We all tend to blame others, even when our own actions have been the cause of our greatest ills.'

'The names she called you, my dear,' Mrs Lynford said to her young friend, 'are such as I cannot and will not repeat.'

'There is even talk,' Gideon put in, looking around at the others, 'that she may have had a hand in her father's death from a violent stomach attack.'

'Good God!' Anthea exclaimed. 'Crispin hinted as much to me, but can it be possible?'

'When one has once been a party to one murder,' John informed her, 'a second or even a third becomes no great matter.'

'I have heard soldiers say something similar,' Gideon confessed. 'They tell me that the face of the first man you kill on the battlefield is for ever burned into your memory. You hesitate for a moment before using your gun or bayonet, and then you do what must be done to survive. After that, all other faces are unremarkable.'

It was almost certain that Georgina had killed her father in order to receive her inheritance while she and her husband were young enough to enjoy its benefits. Yew berries were the suspected agent, although it was impossible to prove.

'I believe,' Lydia told Anthea, 'that she intended to do the same to you when she invited you for tea.'

'A veritable Lady Macbeth!' Rachel exclaimed.

'Surely she would not have done anything so rash,' Anthea objected, her voice more subdued.

'Why not?' Lydia shrugged, her practical, unromantic nature asserting itself. 'You would have gone home, and an hour or so later you would have become seriously ill. It is unlikely that anyone but ourselves would have linked your death with your visit to the Flitwicks. But she is a criminal whose actions are clearly founded on emotion rather than logic. She took risks which could easily have exposed her on several occasions, but her luck held.'

'Until Lydia and John Savidge came to town,' Anthea pointed out.

'She doubtless assumed that she was above suspicion simply because she was Georgina Flitwick.'

'I am eternally grateful that you insisted on accompanying my wife that afternoon,' Gideon said, taking Anthea's hand in his but looking at Lydia with an intensity which expressed his feelings even more than his words did.

'What I do not understand,' Rachel wondered aloud, 'is why Chittering went back into service, if he had received a large amount of money from the sale of the jewels.'

'Alas,' John answered, wagging his index finger, 'one of his many sins was a predilection for gaming. He lived like a prince for more than a year, but his luck turned abruptly and he once more found himself penniless. He took a position with the Griffens, whom he repaid by murdering them much as he had done to Nancy.'

'That is a story I know all too well,' Anthea attested with a sigh. 'Papa was either plump in the pocket or blown up at point nonplus. It is a precarious life at best.'

'Your father seems like a reformed character.' Her husband squeezed the hand he still held. 'I encountered him on Milsom Street this morning and he was more than civil to me!'

'I think his lady friend has had a beneficial influence upon him,' Rachel said. 'He was quite gallant the day that we met them at the Pump Room.'

'By the bye, I have something of particular interest to show you all.' Gideon, producing a folded piece of paper from the inner pocket of his coat, had the air of a conjurer extracting a dove from a hat.

'What is it?' Everyone was agog to know the import of such an inconspicuous object.

His friend in Bristol had rummaged through a collection of old papers and discovered the very letter signed by Miss Shields, which commissioned a copy of the infamous necklace. It was proof positive that Chittering's confession, made almost on the eve of his execution, was not spurious.

Not that any of them had doubted it, but this showed that Georgina had been in possession of the fake jewels since very soon after the so-called theft.

In the meantime, it transpired that Crispin had departed Bath with his little boy — who was, perhaps, the only innocent party in the whole business, and for whom Anthea felt a keen regret at the revelations which would be a burden felt by him and his father for many years to come. John Savidge expressed the opinion that, as Captain Flitwick was now in control of his wife's fortune, a goodly sum was likely to be paid to ensure that Georgina was not hanged but exiled to Botany Bay.

Anthea's own fortunes were now in the ascendant. Many who had refused to speak to her, or who formerly passed her by without a glance, competed with each other in their effusive greetings and awkward apologies. Her innocence could not now be questioned, and though there were those so high in the instep that they would still avoid contact with her for the unforgivable crime of eloping with one of the tribe of Judah, the majority of her neighbours were eager to put the past behind them and restore both their friendship and her good name at once.

She was relieved that she had at last been vindicated, but as her happiness rested mainly in her husband's trust and affection, she did not allow her new elevation to overwhelm her. She was thankful to God for her husband's love and for the friendship and the extraordinary talents of John and Lydia. After a long season of despair and neglect, she had now entered a time of celebration and discovery. The following day gave her even more reason to celebrate.

* * *

The day dawned with a crystal clarity upon the mellowed stone of Bath, lending a golden glow to the majestic crescents and bustling streets of the city on the Avon. Anthea awoke to the deep, low sound of her husband's breathing beside her, and all was well with her world. Later in the morning, her husband left the house on a matter of business, and Anthea once again chaperoned her stepdaughter on a walk in the direction of the Pump Room.

On the way, they encountered Quentin, who had been on his way to their house, but immediately changed direction to accompany the two ladies. Soon after their arrival there, Rachel spied Miss Quimby and deserted her two companions in order to hear the latest *on-dits* from her friend.

'I hate to stand stupidly about like this,' Anthea remarked to Quentin when they were alone.

'It is not so great a burden if one has a charming companion with whom to converse,' he said with light gallantry.

'Do not waste your flummery on me, young man,' she smiled at him, adopting the attitude of an elderly matron. 'Save your cozening words for Rachel.'

'Tell me, ma'am,' he began with a certain degree of diffidence, 'do you think that I would have a favourable reception if I were to ask your husband whether I might be permitted to pay my addresses to Miss Rodrigo?'

She opened her eyes very wide and gave him a considering look.

'My husband is not the one whose objections should concern you.' She turned her head, directing his attention toward the young lady in question. 'What do you think Rachel will say?'

'Will I sound like a confirmed coxcomb if I say that I am confident that she returns my affections?'

'I think you are far too sensible to go so far as to offer for a young lady if you were not reasonably sure of her.'

'Thank you, ma'am.'

'Yes,' she murmured, 'I suspect that you will very likely be enfolded in the bosom of the Rodrigo family.'

'It is my greatest ambition.' He gave a slight bow.

'Whatever are you two smiling about?'

This impertinent question came from Rachel, who had flitted away from Miss Quimby, that young lady having little to relate, and returned to them before they were quite aware.

'I was merely remarking,' Quentin said with the easy prevarication of a born politician, 'what a fine family the Rodrigos are.'

'Indeed we must be,' she quizzed him, 'for you never seem to tire of us.'

'Who could ever be tired of *you*, my dear Miss Rodrigo?'

'Any number of people, I assure you,' Anthea said, forestalling Rachel.

'You will never make a proper and docile young lady of me,' the younger woman said saucily, 'in spite of your heroic efforts.'

'And your papa depended on me to reform you.' Her air of mock disappointment was a treat to behold.

'Where is Mr Rodrigo?' Quentin asked her.

'Conferring with a business associate, I believe.'

'I am amazed,' Mr Safford commented, 'that either of you can bear to be separated for even such a brief time.'

'You have overset all the accepted rules of marriage, Thea.' Rachel was inclined to be censorious.

'How so?'

'The usual custom,' she explained, 'is to fall in love with a gentleman, marry him, and then fall out of love with him.'

'And into love with someone else,' Quentin added.

'Exactly so.' Rachel seemed pleased with his quick understanding. 'But by falling in love *after* your marriage, you have set everything at naught! It is really quite vexatious, for you are generally a pattern-card of propriety.'

'But only consider,' Anthea said with an expressive wave of the hand as she entered into this playful banter, 'that, by reversing the first part of your equation and waiting until after marriage to fall in love with my husband, I can dispense with the last part altogether and not fall *out* of love with him at all.'

They very soon quit the Pump Room, having encountered no one of real interest. Having left that morning as a duo, it was now a trio who returned to the house, where they found that Gideon was at home and was even now closeted in his study again.

'I believe,' Anthea addressed Quentin with a sly look, 'that you expressed a wish to speak with my husband in private, sir?'

'What can you have to say to Papa?' Rachel wondered aloud.

'No doubt,' Anthea adopted the demeanour of an oracle, 'all will be revealed very soon now.'

'Now you are both quizzing me!' Rachel complained. 'I shall have to flounce up the stairs — if I can recall how to flounce.'

'An excellent idea,' Quentin assured her. 'And one most suitable to a young lady.'

'You are quite horrid — the pair of you.' She sniffed and ascended the stairs with a very fair approximation of a feminine flounce.

'Well,' Quentin drew a deep breath and walked over to the study door, 'Nothing ventured, nothing gained!'

'I'm sure that you have little to fear.'

He knocked firmly at the door and was bidden to enter. Anthea, meanwhile, made her own way upstairs, without a flounce but with a heart lighter than it had ever been before.

CHAPTER TWENTY-SEVEN:
IN WHICH ALL IS CONCLUDED

There was never any real doubt that Quentin would be successful in his endeavour. Gideon truly liked and admired the young man, Rachel was more in love with him than she cared to show, and it was not long before all of Bath knew that the Jew's daughter would soon be marrying into a titled family. It was indeed a season of wonders!

John and Lydia returned to Sussex, inviting the Rodrigos to visit them at their earliest convenience. With all the talk of Georgina's imprisonment, trial and subsequent transportation to Australia, as well as speculation on when and where Miss Rodrigo was to be married, both Anthea and Gideon were eager to accept the invitation to Bellefleur, their country estate near Diddlington in Sussex, escaping the whispers and conjectures swirling around them. Hopefully the speculative tittle-tattle would have abated somewhat by the time of their return.

So it was that the commodious house formerly belonging to Sir Hector Mannington was hosting a larger party of visitors than it had done in many a year. The residents, of course, included Lydia's aunt and uncle, the Comte and Comtesse d'Almain, and their young son, Phillip, who had recently marked his first milestone. Now, with the addition of the three Rodrigos and the young man who was soon to marry into the family, it was quite a lively household.

The fields and hills, streams and forests of the area were a welcome respite from the city. All seemed to be tranquillity and harmony, although John and Lydia entertained them with tales of their first adventure, when they had assisted in the capture of a band of smugglers and an avaricious killer who once resided in this very house. There was no trace of violence now, and it all sounded like a story from a past long gone, though it had been a mere three years since the events which they related.

* * *

One evening, after an animated game of charades, which the clever younger couple won easily, but was more an excuse for laughter and frivolity, everyone retired for an early night. It had been a strenuous day, with a long walk through Wyckham Wood and back again, and Anthea and Gideon were eager to spend some time alone together.

'Just think,' Anthea said, casting aside her dressing gown and slipping into bed beside him, 'if it had not been for Georgina, I might well have married Crispin! Is it wrong,' she added, 'to feel a certain gratitude for what she did, horrible as it was?'

'I know what you mean,' Gideon answered her. 'I cannot imagine what I would have done had I met you as a married woman. But still, it was cruel to have put you through seven years of something like imprisonment.'

'It was better so,' she said decisively.

'How can you continue to believe that?'

'Those years made me a better person than I had ever been before. There is nothing like trials and travails to strengthen character. And, in the words of a novel I have read recently, nothing will erode one's morals like an extended season of *health, wealth, ease and tranquillity.*'

'I do not believe that your character needed any improvement.' Gideon refused to be persuaded. 'And I venture to say that all the wealth and ease I can give to you will never make you any less lovely and sweet than you have always been.'

'I sometimes feel,' she said, her head resting on her husband's shoulder, 'that I have wandered into the most beautiful dream. My life is so different from what it was five mere months ago.'

'My most cherished dream,' he confessed, caressing her warm body and drawing her closer still, 'came true on the night that we married.'

'And now,' she whispered against his lips, 'we have a lifetime of love to share.'

'And a very large and comfortable bed which cries out for something more strenuous than a few kisses!'

* * *

While they were indulging their more earthy appetites, John and Lydia remained in the great hall, gazing at the elaborately carved heart above the fireplace, and feeling very pleased with themselves. Their friends were clearly enjoying their visit, and all the shadows of their lives seemed to have melted quite away.

'I think,' Lydia said, with a sideways look, 'that we shall have to withdraw a little from our dabbling in murder and other assorted crimes.'

John stared at her, having never heard such a statement from her before. His wife was a young woman whose thirst for adventure and her inquisitive nature, combined with courage and common sense, made her always ready to leap into the most dangerous escapades without hesitation. What, he wondered, was responsible for this sudden change?

'Why do you say that, my dear?'

'Well, Anthea confessed to me this afternoon that in a few months she will be presenting her husband with a very welcome gift.'

'What is it?' he asked, not nearly as quick in domestic matters as in discovering clues to a murder.

'The Rodrigo family will be adding a new member: a son, perhaps, or a second daughter.'

'Indeed!' John's eyebrows rose. 'But how does that affect us?'

'Well . . .' An impish smile tugged at the corners of her lips. 'I confessed to her that you and I would also be adding to our family.'

For a moment John was quite incapable of speech.

'Lydia!' was all he could say when he recovered his voice.

He leapt to his feet, pulled her up out of her seat and directly into his arms, twirling her about in a rather rough manner, before remembering her condition and setting her down gently on the floor.

'Now,' she told him, 'we are about to embark on the ultimate adventure. I think it will be quite enough to satisfy us — for some time, at least.'

'Not for as long as you imagine, I'll wager.'

She laughed. 'Perhaps not.'

'But wait!' He suddenly caught himself up and cast her a mischievous glance. 'We shall have to inform Mrs Wardle-Penfield that she is soon to become a godmother.'

Lydia had quite forgotten this charge which the uncrowned queen of Diddlington society had laid upon them.

'That is a circumstance which I prefer to ignore.' She sighed and shrugged in resignation. 'Well, she will be a fine godparent, I do not doubt. And one dare not refuse her.'

'I think she is the one person who makes us both shake in our shoes.'

'I have often wondered why no one has ever murdered her,' Lydia said rather wistfully.

'They would not dare!'

With those words they went up to their bedchamber, leaving the great hall, with its flickering shadows, to await a new chapter in its long and storied history.

THE END

Thank you for reading this book.

If you enjoyed it please leave feedback on Amazon or Goodreads, and if there is anything we missed or you have a question about, then please get in touch. We appreciate you choosing our book.

Founded in 2014 in Shoreditch, London, we at Joffe Books pride ourselves on our history of innovative publishing. We were thrilled to be shortlisted for Independent Publisher of the Year at the British Book Awards.

www.joffebooks.com

We're very grateful to eagle-eyed readers who take the time to contact us. Please send any errors you find to corrections@joffebooks.com. We'll get them fixed ASAP.